"You okay?" she asked.

"Yeah." He let out his breath with a whoosh. "In all the years I watched Atlas apprehend perps, or go into buildings to search for drugs or explosives, I knew he'd be okay. He was well trained but also street-smart. I had to deal with it because that was our job. But there are wild things up here that he's not used to messing with."

Erica lightly rubbed his back before slipping her hand away. "Now what?"

Ben was half tempted to ask her to touch him again, maybe even work out the knots between his shoulder blades, but that wasn't a good idea. Not at all. Besides, he had Atlas to tend to. "Attie, what do you think you're doing? *Hier.*"

Instead of coming to him, Atlas lay down in front of the gate to the wire fence and raised his head in defiance.

Ben ran a hand through his hair. His partner was officially on duty. This was about guarding the henhouse and who was he to deny the dog the chance to work instead of play?

Jenna Mindel lives in Northwest Lower Michigan with her husband and their dogs, where she enjoys the Great Lakes, the outdoors and strong coffee. Her love of fairy tales as a kid paved the way for Jenna to eventually create her own happily-ever-after stories. Her passion grew into writing flawed characters who realize their need to trust God before they can trust each other. Contact Jenna through her website, www.jennamindel.com, or at PO Box 2075, Petoskey, MI 49770.

Books by Jenna Mindel

Love Inspired

Second Chance Blessings

A Secret Christmas Family
The Nanny Next Door
Finding Their Way Back

Maple Springs

Falling for the Mom-to-Be
A Soldier's Valentine
A Temporary Courtship
An Unexpected Family
Holiday Baby
A Soldier's Prayer

Visit the Author Profile page at LoveInspired.com for more titles.

Finding Their Way Back

Jenna Mindel

If you purchased this book without a cover you should be aware that this book is stolen property. It was reported as "unsold and destroyed" to the publisher, and neither the author nor the publisher has received any payment for this "stripped book."

LOVE INSPIRED®
INSPIRATIONAL ROMANCE

Recycling programs for this product may not exist in your area.

ISBN-13: 978-1-335-59710-6

Finding Their Way Back

Copyright © 2023 by Jenna Mindel

All rights reserved. No part of this book may be used or reproduced in any manner whatsoever without written permission except in the case of brief quotations embodied in critical articles and reviews.

This is a work of fiction. Names, characters, places and incidents are either the product of the author's imagination or are used fictitiously. Any resemblance to actual persons, living or dead, businesses, companies, events or locales is entirely coincidental.

For questions and comments about the quality of this book, please contact us at CustomerService@Harlequin.com.

Love Inspired
22 Adelaide St. West, 41st Floor
Toronto, Ontario M5H 4E3, Canada
www.LoveInspired.com

Printed in U.S.A.

Therefore if any man be in Christ,
he is a new creature: old things are passed away;
behold, all things are become new.

—*2 Corinthians* 5:17

Thank you, Colleen Dittmar, for your insight into what it's like to be a hospital RN. I'd also like to thank Susie Duquette and Kelly December for sharing what it takes for a dog to become a therapy dog and the impact these wonderful animals have. I really appreciate everyone's time and knowledge.

I'd also like to thank my editor, Shana Asaro, for her wisdom on how to make this book finally come together. You rock!

Chapter One

Erica Laine wasn't about to spend her forty-ninth birthday alone. Her two grown daughters had called and sent cards, and even a large bouquet of flowers had arrived on her doorstep, but that wasn't the same as celebrating in person. Nothing was as good as in person, and Erica missed being part of a family.

She should be used to being alone by now. Erica had felt alone long before her husband of twenty-seven years died last year. Dr. Robert Laine had had complications from a debilitating stroke he'd suffered three years prior, two years before he'd planned to retire at sixty-two. They were supposed to travel the globe, she and Bob.

Erica peered out the window of the four-bedroom, three-and-a-half-bath home situated on an acre between her hometown of Pine and the city of Marquette in the Upper Peninsula of Michigan. It wouldn't be long before the next chapter in her life would soon be written. Adventures beckoned her and she could hardly wait. Finally, she was leaving her hometown.

"I'm going to travel, Bob. Not like we'd planned, but at least I'll see more of this country."

She'd sold her husband's house after living here for too long. Even though she'd included most of the furnishings with the sale, there was still a lot to sort through. Everyone had said to wait at least a year after Bob's death before making any big changes. She wished she hadn't listened.

Reminders of her husband were everywhere—at work, home and even in the community. He'd donated a portion of his investments for an ongoing medical scholarship at Pine High School. She'd had to paste on a smile for that event. She should have cut ties and moved beyond the memories here sooner. Both the good and bad.

Erica watched as a pop-up rainstorm caused little rivers of water to stream down her driveway. A quick flash of lightning, followed by a drawn-out rumble of thunder, made Erica smile. She loved summer thunderstorms. Slipping into her rain slicker, she headed out the door. She was meeting two friends for lunch whom she hadn't seen in weeks, and couldn't wait to hear how they'd both been.

It didn't take long to drive to the Pine Inn Café. By the time Erica parked, the July sun had come back out with a vengeance. Steam rose from the wet pavement, making the log-cabin hotel and restaurant look romantic and maybe even a little mysterious, like some wild place in a rugged movie set instead of a small Upper Peninsula town.

Getting out of her car, Erica stripped off her slicker and threw it in the passenger seat. She took a moment to tip back her head and bask in the sudden heat of the sun.

"Hey, Erica!" Maddie Williams—no, she was Maddie Taylor now—waved.

Erica caught up to her young friend, also a widow,

who'd remarried the month before. "How's it feel to be married, what…three weeks now?"

Maddie's bright smile spoke for itself. "Wonderful. Of course one of those weeks was spent in the Bahamas, so how could it be anything less?"

"I'm so happy for you." Erica meant it.

Her twenty-five-year-old friend was the same age as Erica's oldest daughter, yet a tough first marriage had made Maddie seem much older.

"Me too." Maddie smiled. She no longer wore the big glasses she used to hide behind. She'd gained clarity along with the contacts she wore regularly now.

At church, Erica had gotten to know the man Maddie had married. Jackson Taylor led the worship team and he had roped Maddie into singing. Erica had had no idea Maddie possessed such a beautiful voice. Her friend positively glowed these days, and Erica knew it wasn't only from her honeymoon tan.

They entered the restaurant together and met Ruth Miller-Harris, also widowed, and newly married to her business partner. Both women had been blessed with second chances at love with strong men of faith. Erica tamped down the pinch of envy that stung her heart. Surely, she was too old for such longings. She slipped into a seat at their usual table in the back overlooking the Pine Inn Café gardens.

"Happy birthday!" Ruth pushed a wrapped box toward her. "We both picked it out."

"Thank you." Erica picked it up, eager. "Should I open it now?"

"Definitely." Maddie gripped her hands together as if she'd open the box if Erica didn't.

Erica used a butter knife to break the frilly ribbon and

then tore away the wrapping paper. After glancing first at Maddie, then Ruth, she opened the box. A leather-bound book was lying inside. The words *Wherever you go, go with your heart* were etched into the soft cover with swirls and filigree.

She lifted the book out of the box and opened it, realizing it was a travel journal, complete with pockets to stash mementos and protective pages for photographs, along with blank pages for journaling. A leather-encased writing pen was tucked inside, as well.

Erica felt her throat tighten. Her husband would have loved keeping track of their trips to reminisce over later. This was the kind of thing he might have given her. "This is such a thoughtful gift—thank you!"

Ruth smiled. "We found it here in the gift shop the last time we met for lunch, after you told us about applying for the traveling-nurse gig."

Maddie nodded. "When do you leave?"

Erica took a sip of the water their waitress had placed on the table for each of them. "Toward the end of August. The job starts September first."

"Wow, not long. Where's your assignment?" Ruth asked.

"Thirteen weeks in Jackson, Wyoming." It was the usual contract time for traveling nurses, and she'd cover for an ICU nurse on maternity leave. Her temporary licensing for that state was in the works and Erica looked forward to spending fall near the mountains. After that, who knew where she'd end up next.

"Where are you going to stay?" Ruth asked.

"I'm not sure. I was thinking of buying a camper, but with the possibility of snow, that might not be a good idea. There are year-round campgrounds in Jackson that have cabins, but that might be too costly." Financially, Erica was pretty much set, but still, she wasn't one to waste money if she didn't have to. She also didn't want to cart around a bunch of stuff to move into an apartment, or even a cabin, for only three months.

"What about a tiny home?" Maddie set down her menu. "I just saw an advertisement in the Marquette newspaper about a local tiny-home builder. Superior something-or-other. Google it."

"Maybe I will." Erica grinned.

She'd seen shows on cable TV about tiny-home living and had always thought it a cool concept. She had her late husband's hefty pickup truck, so towing it shouldn't be a problem once she learned how. But could she get one built in time?

She wouldn't know unless she made that call and asked.

Fifty years old and I'm back home living with my parents.

Ben Fisher got up from his mother's kitchen table after lingering over a cup of coffee. It had been a long time since he'd sat there. Much too long. "Thanks for lunch."

She gave him a hug. "Thanks for coming home."

"Of course." It made sense to come here, where he'd grown up, before figuring out the rest of his life.

Atlas, his K-9 partner, barked for attention. The dog had retired from the force with him.

His mom bent to give the dog a pat. "You, too, handsome."

"Back to work." Ben stretched. "Come on, Attie."

The ten-year-old Belgian Malinois had been with him for eight years while they worked in the Grand Rapids

Police Department. Together, they'd helped the bomb squad search for explosives at Van Andel Arena and stood watch as government dignitaries and even presidential candidates had used the space. Attie had been his partner on patrol, too, and could sniff out narcotics with the best of them. He and Atlas had had some close calls, and Ben owed his life to the dog.

Atlas nudged his mother's golden retriever as if asking her to follow them, but Millie was old and stayed put on the memory-foam dog bed. Atlas gave up on Millie and followed Ben out the door with a high-pitched yip. He wanted to play, so Ben threw the ball he carried in his construction belt. The dog needed new purpose as much as Ben. Atlas was used to working, and transitioning to retired life might not be easy for either of them.

Ben had moved back to his hometown of Pine, Michigan, a few weeks ago to help his son's tiny-home construction business get off the ground. Ben's parents had a small hobby farm and they had let Jason, their grandson, take over one of the outbuildings as a workshop. Ben couldn't be more proud of his son for forging his own path by starting a business. Jason understood Ben's need for hands-on work, now more than ever, and had invited his help.

"About time," Ben's son called out.

Ben threw the ball a second time for Atlas. "I don't move as fast as I used to."

Jason shook his head. "Yeah, right. You're in great shape, Dad."

Evidently, his ex-wife hadn't thought so. He'd never forget how she'd dropped the bombshell of wanting a [illegible]orce by serving him papers seven months ago, right [illegible] they'd put up the Christmas tree. She had fallen for someone else and wanted to get on with her life. What irritated Ben the most was that Lori had the gall to tell him he'd find somebody new if he'd only look. Ben didn't want to *look*. He didn't want somebody new to lose. He'd wanted to stay married to Lori even though they'd drifted apart. Even though their failed marriage was mostly his fault for staying closed-off and guarded.

At least Lori had given back her wedding rings, which had been his grandmother's. Ben planned to give the set to his daughter, Molly, if she wanted them. His wedding band would go to Jason. Ben had taken that off when the divorce was final.

"Yo, Dad. You there?"

Ben shook off his thoughts. "Sorry, what did you say?"

"I've got to run to the lumber store."

"Sure, no problem." Ben had some sanding to do on the cupboards of a home they were finishing up. Sand, then stain.

Jason touched his shoulder. "You okay?"

Ben laughed, but he didn't sound amused. More like a wounded bear. "I will be."

His son squeezed his shoulder. "I'll be back in, like, an hour."

"I'll be here." Nowhere else to go.

Atlas nipped at his heels. He wanted the ball thrown again, so Ben obliged.

His son climbed into his truck and pulled away. The divorce hadn't been easy for Jason or Molly. They hadn't wanted to take sides and Ben didn't want them to. Ben knew Jason kept in touch with Lori, and Ben wouldn't want it any other way. His ex-wife had been a good mom. Lori had tried to be a good wife, too, but Ben hadn't been the easiest husband.

Blowing out his breath, he got to work. And then the phone rang. Jason had forgotten to take his phone.

"Superior Tiny Homes." Ben answered his son's cell, the only number listed for the business.

"Hi." A woman's voice was on the other end. "Do you have an inventory?"

Ben nearly laughed. They were not an RV dealer. Other than a small tiny home that had been roughed in, then abandoned, they had nothing. "We build to order."

"How long does it take?" She had a pleasant voice. Not too high or low. Nice and smooth-sounding. Soothing even.

"That depends on a lot of things." Ben wasn't really sure how long it took. A lot depended on the order and Jason handled all that. "My son is the one you'll want to talk to. I can have him call you."

"Hmm, maybe I could stop by? Is this afternoon a good time?"

Ben gazed out the open garage door toward the fields that had been cut for hay a couple of weeks ago. They looked golden instead of green, dried by the hot sun. Today's brief rain hadn't done much to drench the beautiful swath of land his dad still cut, baled and put up for hay. He sold most of it, but some bales were kept for his mother's chickens. "Sure. This afternoon will be fine, say an hour and a half from now?"

"That works."

"Do you need directions?"

"I'll get the address off your website." The woman had a smile in her voice.

"Sounds good. See you then." After disconnecting, Ben got the distinct feeling he'd heard that woman's voice before, but he couldn't quite place it.

Her voice lingered in his mind long after the call, sounding way too familiar, like he should know it…

No way it's her.

That voice couldn't belong to the girl he'd wanted to marry before he became a cop. They'd been engaged, but Erica had wanted to wait until she finished nursing school. And then she'd met this doctor, a man fifteen years older than her, and that had been the end of them.

Ben figured that moving home after all these years, he'd run into a lot of folks he'd once known. He couldn't help it that Erica Moore still lurked in his dreams on occasion. Though she was Erica Laine now and had been for years. He was bound to run into her one of these days; might as well rip off that old bandage now and get it over with.

Ben scratched the back of his neck. The only two women he'd ever loved in his life had left him for other men. Lori had said that he'd never really been there for her. That was probably true. His coworkers used to call him *RoboCop* because he carried out his duties in an even-keeled, emotionless way. Ben had learned long ago, when his first assigned partner and best friend had been killed right in front of him, that *feelings* didn't get the job done. In fact, feeling too much paralyzed him.

Atlas dropped the ball at Ben's feet and barked.

"Good boy." Ben picked it up.

Attie understood him better than he did sometimes. He needed to get away from these dark thoughts. One more throw and then Ben would get to work sanding those cupboards.

Erica drove from her house toward an address she hadn't visited in a long time. A place just down the road from the house where she grew up. The drive was as pretty as ever, with gentle hills and long stretches of daisy-dotted meadows that flowed into miniforests of pine and hardwoods.

At the long driveway, she stopped and double-checked the address on her phone, verifying it against the company website. This place used to belong to Ben Fisher's parents, but maybe they'd sold it.

She pulled in and followed the sign for Superior Tiny Homes, then took a sharp left away from the white farmhouse surrounded by a white split-rail fence and the bright red barn just beyond. Everything looked the same as she remembered with the exception of a newer, red pole barn and a fully set-up tiny home not far from it. Surely, Ben Fisher's parents were not builders of tiny homes. Ben's dad had to be in his seventies by now.

She parked near the pole barn and stared at the home to the left of it. A cute little place with a wooden wraparound deck and shutters that had pine-tree cutouts. If that tiny home was any indication of the handiwork here, then she was in good hands.

Erica cut the truck's engine and got out. She walked toward the pole barn and was met by a handsome young man who looked to be in his midtwenties.

"Hi, I'm Jason Fisher. Did you call about a tiny home?"

Erica stared at the boy, and then extended her hand. "I did. Are you related to Ben Fisher, perchance?"

Jason smiled and Erica knew that he was. He had Ben's smile. "That's my dad. He'll be out in a few. What can I help you with?"

Erica's ears tingled and her stomach tipped and rolled. She hadn't seen Ben Fisher since the day she ended their engagement all those years ago. If she *had* married Ben

Fisher instead of Robert Laine, this young man in front of her might have been her son.

That young man waited for her to speak.

Erica pulled herself back to the present and smiled. "I'd like to purchase a tiny home that I can pull with that truck and live in during cold months."

Jason glanced at her truck. "Is that a Super Duty?"

"Yes. A Ford F-250." Her late husband had purchased it four years ago, before his stroke, in preparation to buy that camper they'd wanted.

"You'll do fine. Come on into the office and tell me about your plans and we'll see what fits."

She followed Ben's son into the pole barn that had big open doors on both ends. Country music played from a radio on a shelf. Inside was a tiny home in the final stages of being built. It looked pretty big to her. There was no way she'd haul something like that across the country. She entered a corner room that had a desk, three chairs, a computer and a small window that was open. The warm summer breeze played with the papers on the desk.

Jason shoved those papers under a hammer. "Okay, let's get started. How do you plan to use the tiny home?"

"I'll be a traveling nurse this September in Jackson, Wyoming. After that, I'm not sure where I'll be needed, so I'd like something easy to tow."

"September, you say?"

"I need to leave no later than August twenty-fifth, but a little earlier would be much better." Erica had about thirty days to remain in her house after the closing papers were signed in two weeks, give or take a couple of days.

Jason leaned back in his chair behind the desk, across from her. "That timeline might be tough to meet. I have a couple of orders ahead of yours."

Erica bit her lip. She'd like to give Ben's son the business. "So you have nothing in stock?"

"No." Jason chuckled, then leaned forward. "Although, I do have a small one that is already roughed in. Would you like to see it?"

"Absolutely." Erica followed Ben's son through the pole-barn workshop and through another open garage door to a simply built pavilion. Underneath it was parked a seriously tiny home. He hadn't been kidding when he'd called it *small.*

"So this was built in the spring but the buyers backed out. It's not complete, but we might be able to fit it in between our other projects."

Erica needed a more definitive answer than *might*, but she'd hear him out. The tiny home looked like a tall shed on wheels, although she'd never seen a shed with a little dormer. The roof wasn't on and neither was the siding. She ran her hand over plywood. Smaller would mean easier to tow and, more importantly, back up into place. Of course, she'd have to practice. A lot.

"Let's go inside." Jason opened the full-size, windowed door and stepped in.

Erica followed.

The inside surprised her, looking roomier than she'd thought. Glancing up at the high ceiling, she spotted a loft. That explained the dormers.

Jason followed her gaze. "A queen-size mattress will fit nicely up there."

Erica could use the full-size mattress from her daughter's old room to give her more space, but how would she get up there? Surely, they'd build some steps.

Then he pointed at a framed-off room. "This is the bathroom."

Erica laughed at the broom-closet size. "You're kidding."

Jason smiled. "We can get a full bathroom set up in here. Smaller fixtures, sure, but it'll get the job done."

"Wow." Erica looked around. "I think this might work."

Jason nodded. "With your truck and the proper hitch setup, you'd have no problem towing it. Let's go back to the office and consider pricing and interior items. I can show you the original plans, but we can make some alterations based on your preferences if you choose to move forward."

"Thank you." Erica exited down the steps and turned to follow Jason back to the little office when she saw him.

Ben Fisher stood in the field with a large dog dancing at his heels. The dog looked like a German shepherd but with less hair. The coloring was more of a lighter tan and his muzzle and ears were a soft brown. He had a white spot in the center of his chest, too. A beautiful animal.

She watched as the first man she'd ever loved threw a tennis ball for the dog. Ben stood a little over six feet and still looked as strong as an oak. His shoulders were broader than she remembered. He'd filled out some, too. The navy T-shirt he was wearing clung to muscular arms, and for a moment or two, Erica couldn't look away.

But then he spotted her and scowled.

All good things come to an end.

Erica waved.

The dog dropped the ball and stared at it, waiting for Ben to pick it back up. He did, and then the dog danced around him, yipping again.

"Here's my dad." Jason waited for Ben to join them.

The dog looked up at them and then bounded for her.

She took a step back, feeling nervous, but the friendly expression on the dog's face made her keep still.

"Attie, halt."

The dog stopped.

When Ben was next to the dog, he gently said, *"Langsam."*

It sounded like *laung-sum*. What did that mean?

The dog walked slowly toward her. His paws were huge, but his face looked so sweet and his big brown eyes were gentle.

Erica crouched down and extended her hand for the dog to sniff.

He licked her fingers.

Still crouched, Erica petted the dog's head and scratched behind his ears. "He's beautiful. What's his name?"

"Atlas. Attie for short."

"A fine name." Erica stood and faced the man she'd once been engaged to. "Hello, Ben."

"Erica. You here to buy a tiny home?" He no longer scowled, but his hazel eyes looked stone-cold. His light brown hair was liberally streaked with gray, but that made him more handsome rather than less.

"I hope so."

Attie nudged under her hand for another pet. He also sat on her foot.

Erica laughed and obliged the dog.

Jason looked from his dad to Erica and then back. "So you two know each other?"

We grew up with each other. Erica waited for Ben to explain, but he didn't say a thing, so she kept her answer vague. "We went to school together."

"Oh." Jason narrowed his eyes, then shrugged. "Cool. Well, let's take a look at those plans."

Erica followed Ben's son, and Ben's dog followed her.

When she sat down, Attie lay at her feet. Erica patted his head. "You're a good boy."

Jason smiled. "He really likes you."

"I like him, too." Erica had always loved dogs.

She turned toward the large sheets of paper Jason unrolled. All the lines made it a little hard for her to understand what she was looking at.

He turned the computer screen her way, then clicked on a couple of spots, and in moments a floor plan of the tiny home she'd just toured came to life in 3D. "Okay, here's what we have."

Erica listened to him explain the options and price, and soon, she could see the possibilities, but the time frame was still tight. It was a lot to take in, especially since Erica was acutely aware of Ben working on the bigger home only feet away. Why was he here? Last she knew, he lived in Grand Rapids and worked as a police officer.

"Well? Do you want to take this information, look it over and then let me know?"

Erica knew that would be wise, but something about the tall little shed with dormers called to her. She needed a traveling home and it needed an owner. "Is it just you and your dad building these?"

Jason smiled. "Yeah. It's hard to find good help."

Erica knew that was a problem everywhere, and had an idea. "I'd like to stay with the original options, but I'd like to propose an idea to guarantee it's finished on time."

"What's that?"

"What if I worked with you to get it done?" Erica bit her lip, waiting for his response.

"Huh. Interesting." Jason tapped the pen he was holding against his lips. "Do you have any construction experience?"

"Not a lick, but I can learn. I'm available to work two full days a week. Wednesdays, Thursdays or Fridays. You choose."

"If you're willing to take the minimum hourly wage, considering we'd have to teach you everything, I'd say we have a deal."

Erica grinned. "You can take it off the final price if you'd rather, so it won't affect your payroll and all that."

Jason laughed. "My payroll is me and my dad. Although, he refused his last paycheck, so I'm banking them."

That was generous of Ben, but then, parents did a lot for their kids. "Will he mind?"

Jason looked amused. "He'll be fine."

Remembering that frown, Erica wasn't so sure. She didn't want to cause any problems between a father and son. "Maybe we should ask him."

Jason waved away her concern. "Trust me, he's fine. Besides, it's my decision to make. Now, let's look over those options you're agreeing to one last time."

Erica nodded, but her mind wandered. If Ben wasn't an owner of Superior Tiny Homes, what was he doing up here?

Jason pushed a paper in front of her that listed everything the previous buyers had wanted. "So you've known my dad a long time."

"I grew up just down the road." Erica had ridden the bus with Ben and their friendship started when he'd come to her rescue. A couple of older boys were picking on her and Ben stepped in. He'd only been eleven at the time. She was ten.

The memory of Ben, fierce even at a young age, made Erica smile. Until Bob Laine entered her life, there had only been Ben. Always Ben. She sometimes wondered what her life might have been like had she stayed with him. She'd loved Bob, but Ben had always hovered in the back of her thoughts. In her heart—

"Okay, Erica, if you'll sign here. And I'll need a check as a down payment to get started."

Erica shut down her errant thoughts and signed her name, then dug in her purse for her checkbook. She wrote out the agreed-upon amount and handed it over.

"We're all set, then. How's Wednesdays and Thursdays sound for your days on the job?" He handed her another piece of paper. "Job application. Fill it out and bring it with you Wednesday."

"Sounds perfect." Erica stood and extended her hand. "Thank you, Jason."

He stood as well and shook her hand. "Let's tell my father you're coming on board."

Erica's stomach rolled over. What if he wasn't fine with it? What then? She followed Ben's son into the shop area with heavy steps.

"Hey, Dad." Jason actually grinned and there was mischief lurking in his eyes. "Erica's going to help us finish up her tiny home."

Erica watched Ben closely, but he didn't give much away. Only his hazel eyes reflected a flash of fire that was quickly extinguished. Just as she'd feared, he wasn't happy about the arrangement.

"An extra pair of hands should help" was all Ben said.

"Yeah. Well, I gotta run over to my house a minute." Jason started walking away. Fast. But then he called out, "Erica, show up Wednesday around nine."

"Sure." Erica stood there feeling like she should ask

Ben if he minded, but this was his son's business, his son's decision. "Well, I should probably head home, too."

"Okay."

Erica wanted to say something—anything—that might ease the tension between them, but came up empty. "Okay, then. Bye, Ben. See you Wednesday."

"Erica."

She walked out and climbed into her truck, started it and backed up. She waved as she pulled away, and sure enough, Ben still had the same frown on his face.

Wednesday promised to be interesting for sure.

Chapter Two

Ben watched Erica pull away. Why had Jason agreed to let her work with them? What did she know about building anything, and how on earth would he teach her when half the time he sought direction from his son?

"She put a deposit on that abandoned tiny home." Jason had crept up behind him.

"That's good." He was trying not to react outwardly to his inner turmoil at seeing her after all these years.

She'd aged beautifully. Her rich brown hair didn't have any gray and her dark eyes were still expressive. Sure, she had a few more lines around those eyes he used to get lost in, but then who didn't? She looked thinner than he remembered, but still fit. Erica had been a runner in high school. Had she kept it up?

"Is she an old girlfriend or something?" Jason asked.

"Something like that." Ben headed back to the workshop. He had some sanding to do.

His son pushed his shoulder. "Come on, Dad, what's the story? You both seemed awkward around each other."

Releasing a heavy sigh, Ben explained, "We were engaged and she broke it off."

"How come?"

Ben shook his head at his nosy son. "Does it really matter?"

Jason shrugged. "Seems like it still matters to you."

It shouldn't, but it did. Maybe because his recent divorce and retirement had him a little raw around the edges. He might be only fifty, but life as he'd known it was over. Changed forever. After twenty-five years of marriage, he was single again. A new and different life stretched before him.

"She left me for someone else," Ben said, grinding out the words.

Jason's smile crumpled. "I'm sorry, Dad."

Ben gave a bitter laugh as he entered the large tiny home. "History has a way of repeating itself."

"Erica said something about a traveling-nurse job. She's headed to Wyoming at the end of August and that's why she wanted a tiny home. She's not still married, is she?"

So Erica was finally leaving Pine. "Her husband died last year. February or March, I think."

"Hmm." Jason grabbed a rag and wiped off the wood cupboards Ben had sanded. "I think we're ready to stain."

Ben nodded. "Just one more door to sand."

"Thanks for coming up here to work with me. It's not easy finding reliable help."

"I know." Ben slapped his son's back to let him know there'd been no harm done with his questions. He imagined some might not like working for someone so young, but Jason knew his trade and knew it well. "It's enjoyable work."

"I'm glad you think so, because now that Erica bought the small one, we'll be up to our ears."

Ben chuckled. "Then we better stop jawing and get to work."

Three tiny-home projects—one nearly done, one not started and finishing the small one—was *up to their ears.* Ben returned to sanding the last cupboard door. He'd always found satisfaction in hands-on work. He'd had a workshop in his garage where he'd tinkered with making furniture. It had been his safe place to escape the rough parts of his job.

His wife had never really liked his creations. Lori had modern taste and said his stuff looked too old and chunky. Out of all the furniture he'd made, Jason had a table, his parents had a bench and the rest was stored in his parents' barn.

His life had taken an odd turn, for sure. He hadn't planned on retiring with Atlas, but once his wife handed him those divorce papers, there was no point in staying in the area. She got the house, he got his furniture and Atlas. And his pension.

He shouldn't have been surprised. He and Lori had been going through the motions for a long while. Ever since he'd checked out emotionally. She deserved better, but then so did he.

"You boys want to take a break?" His mom had entered the workshop with a plate of homemade chocolate-chip cookies.

"Thanks, Grandma." Jason dug right in.

Atlas whined for one, too.

"No chocolate for you, Attie." Ben grabbed a cookie.

His mom offered Atlas a few dog treats from her apron pocket.

"You're spoiling him," Ben warned.

His mother merely smiled. "He deserves a little spoiling. You do, too."

Ben took two more cookies. "Thanks for these."

"Dad, I'm going to grab a water. Do you want one?"

"Sure."

Atlas circled his feet. The treats were gone, but Ben knew the particular yip Attie gave was for the ball to be thrown.

"We've got a deadline here, boy." Ben stepped out of the pole barn and threw the ball as far as he could.

The clients who'd bought the twenty-eight-foot tiny home were picking it up at the end of next week. He and Jason had a lot to do yet, and taking cookie breaks and talking about Erica wasn't getting them any closer to completion.

Erica Laine.

She'd been Erica Moore when they were together. He'd never forgotten her. Never really got over her, either. It was interesting that their paths had crossed again after all these years. He wasn't going to do anything about it. Not only was he not interested in a romantic relationship, but Erica was also leaving Pine. Maybe for good, and he certainly wasn't in the mood to get left. Again.

At the end of the workday, Ben was just shutting the garage door when Jason exited his own tiny house wearing swim trunks and a T-shirt with a beach towel around his neck.

Ben walked toward him, more concerned than maybe he should be about Erica working with them. What if she got hurt? "Do you think it wise to hire a client?"

Jason shrugged. "Erica? She's eager to get her house

done and we really could use the help. Even if she's only a gofer at first."

"I suppose you're right." This was his son's business and it wasn't Ben's place to push too hard on whom Jason hired. Even if Ben hated the idea of seeing the woman who'd once ripped his heart in two on a regular basis.

"'Course I'm right." Jason grinned.

"Where are you headed?" None of his business really, but Ben liked to know.

"Meeting friends at Black Rocks."

"Be careful."

"Always." His son laughed before sliding into his truck.

Ben watched Jason pull out. Black Rocks was a popular destination in Marquette, but especially during the summer months. The natural dark-rock formations were basically cliffs jutting out into Lake Superior. There was a small beach nestled in a rocky cove that created a protected little bay where the water was always warmer, but still downright chilly even in early July. He'd worry about Jason until the kid returned home well after dark on a Friday night. He shouldn't worry, since Jason was a full-grown man capable of taking care of himself, but Ben was his parent. And parents worried.

Ben had frequented Black Rocks when he was much younger than Jason, especially while attending police academy at Northern Michigan University. He'd jumped off those same cliffs like it was nothing. He'd even made the plunge with Erica by his side, holding hands as they leaped into Lake Superior's cold, clear water. They'd explored every inch of that shoreline. They'd explored a lot of places around here in those days.

Memories of the two of them flooded his thoughts and he'd seen Erica only briefly. How much worse would it be working with her? Ben didn't want to go there. He didn't want to *feel*, only to lose someone he cared about once again. Never again. He'd been bruised enough for one lifetime.

"Come on, Attie, let's see what's for dinner." Ben entered his parents' white farmhouse and inhaled the luscious scent of fried peppers and onions. "Smells good."

His mom nodded. "Your father is grilling the brats."

"Anything I can do?" Ben didn't mind cooking. He wasn't great at it, but could make a decent meal.

"Gather up the salad dressings and take them outside. We're eating on the back deck."

Made sense. It had been a glorious summer day and summers were too short in the Upper Peninsula of Michigan. Seemed like as soon as Labor Day came and went, the seasonal switch would flip from warm days to cool. Sultry summer nights to freeze warnings.

He did as his mom asked and joined his father outside. His parents' dog, Millie, was lying in a sunny spot on the deck. Her muzzle and the hair around her eyes were white with age. She didn't move much, but managed to be wherever his parents were.

Once seated around the table with a large canvas umbrella in its center, Ben's mom and dad reached for his hands. Every meal, his father said grace. Ben listened, but the words didn't move him. Nothing moved him. Not anymore.

After the blessing, his dad turned toward him, passing the plate of bratwurst. "Your mom and I have been thinking about giving you half of that back thirty acres."

"That's nice of you." Ben hadn't anticipated this gift so soon. "Why?"

His mom passed him a bowl of homemade potato

salad. "We're getting up there in years, and well, to be honest, we'd love for you to live right here, where we can keep an eye on you."

Ben laughed when his mom winked. They were in their early seventies and both stayed active, but one never knew the future. "Want me to move out, huh?"

It was his mom's turn to laugh. "You know you can stay in the house as long as you like. We have the room, that's for sure. No, we want to divide up that property between you and your brother now, so everything is set."

Ben nodded. He had a brother who lived downstate. Would Brad keep his part of the land or sell it? The house and surrounding five acres had always been separate from the rest of the acreage his parents owned. "Thank you."

"Brad will have his, too, but you get first choice. You're the oldest," his dad clarified.

"And you're here," his mom added.

"Sure." Ben dug into his food.

He hadn't really considered staying in Pine permanently, but maybe he should. His family was here. Over the years, he hadn't visited like a son should have, and by staying, maybe he could make up for lost time with his folks. He'd be close to his son, but far from his daughter. And Lori, which was probably best. He didn't want to run into his ex-wife with her boyfriend. Maybe someday he could, but not now with the wound still fresh.

Ben had always loved it up here, so why not stay? He'd sent Jason and Molly to his parents' for a week or two each summer when they'd been young. Jason had loved it here as well, so it was no surprise that his son had attended Ben's alma mater for construction management.

Ben's daughter would make her mark at a downstate

law school this fall. Molly wanted to be a prosecuting attorney. She was sharp. Molly had her mom's stubborn streak, but also her dad's police-officer heart for justice. She'd do well in the field of law.

Looking at how well his kids had turned out, he shouldn't believe his marriage had been a complete failure. But then, neither of his kids had been surprised by the divorce. That spoke volumes. Lori hadn't been happy and their kids knew it. Too bad Ben hadn't figured that out sooner. She'd wanted to go to counseling years ago, but he'd refused. He didn't open up with loved ones—there was no way he'd spill his guts to some stranger no matter how qualified. Ben had had his fill of the city's job-mandated shrink and that hadn't helped him.

His mom's hand on his interrupted his thoughts. "What are your plans this evening?"

He shrugged. "I'll probably go for a walk with Atlas, why?"

"Your father and I are heading into town to play pickleball. Can you give Millie her meds with a treat if we're not back by nine?"

"Sure, Mom." Ben would rather work on the tiny home, but Jason had been adamant about keeping relatively normal daytime hours because they worked Saturdays. They took Sundays off.

Sundays were when Ben's thoughts ran wild and regrets ran deep. Without hands-on work to keep his mind busy, he usually wound up in a deep funk by the time the day was done. He might be the only man alive who welcomed Monday mornings.

At least a long walk would get him out of the house and give Atlas a way to expend his energy, as well. They'd both sleep better come bedtime.

After helping his mother clean up, Ben grabbed his keys. "Come on, Attie, let's go for a ride."

The dog barked with excitement. He'd always loved going in the car.

Once in Ben's vehicle, they headed for a walking trail that he'd wanted to check out. It wasn't far from home, but he didn't remember ever seeing it before. When they arrived at the trailhead parking lot, Ben got out and let Atlas out, too. There were three other cars parked, as well. They'd have company on the trail.

Checking the trailhead map, he saw that the walking trail was newly donated land that wound through the woods for miles. "Ready, Attie?"

Atlas circled Ben's feet and gave a yip.

"No ball today, buddy. Just walking." With a leash in hand, Ben started down the wood-chip-strewn trail, marveling at how much cooler it felt under the heavy canopy of trees.

Atlas bounded along in front of him.

There was a soothing sense of peace in these woods, and Ben knew he'd bring Atlas here more often. Ferns covered the ground and a soft breeze whispered through the pines and hardwoods. Ben concentrated on the sounds around him—birdsong, and the chatter of red squirrels. Attie seemed relaxed, too, and stepped quietly as if also in contemplation of the nature surrounding them.

And then he saw her.

So much for the peaceful walk.

Erica Laine was jogging right toward him. Dressed in running shorts and a tank top, she had earbuds in and hadn't yet noticed him or Atlas. It gave him a moment to admire her summer tan.

Atlas blew his cover by running straight for Erica.

Her gaze flew to his and then she stopped, pulled out her earbuds and smiled. "Hello."

"Nice night."

"It is." Erica petted Atlas. "Do you come here often?"

"First time."

Erica pointed behind her. "There's an open spot with a big pond, and the trail winds around it. It's really pretty."

"Thanks, we'll check it out." Ben might even throw a few sticks into the water for Atlas.

Erica looked like she wasn't sure whether to go or stay.

He made it easy for her. "Don't let us interrupt your run."

She smiled. "Oh, yeah. Sure. See you Wednesday."

"Yup." He stepped aside so she could continue down the trail.

He watched her run a few steps and then blew out his breath. Nothing would soothe him now.

Sunday morning, Erica couldn't wait to tell Ruth and Maddie about her tiny-home purchase. She'd stayed up late the night before after her twelve-hour shift at the hospital and researched tiny-home blogs online. She'd viewed all sorts of interiors for ideas on what she'd need and what she wouldn't. It was daunting, but exhilarating at the same time. She was finally stepping out on her very own adventure.

Walking into the foyer of her church, she spotted Ruth and Maddie near the coffee table and rushed toward them. "Hey."

"Morning, Erica," Maddie said.

Ruth sipped her coffee. "You look happy."

"I'm thrilled. I bought a tiny home from that place Maddie told us about—Superior Tiny Homes." Erica reached for a heavy paper cup and filled it with hot black coffee.

"That's wonderful."

"'Course, it's only half-built, so I'm going to work there to help finish it in time."

Ruth tipped her head. "Have you ever done anything like this before?"

Erica shrugged. "No, but there's people who build their own tiny homes with no previous experience, so how hard can it be?"

Maddie and Ruth shared a look.

And Erica laughed. "Okay, I know it'll be a challenge, but I'm working with the owner who builds them, and he sure seems to know what he's doing. I'll be in good hands."

Erica thought about Ben's strong hands. Was he still married? She didn't think to look for a ring. Not that it mattered. She wasn't interested in renewing their relationship, other than as friendship. The fact that he was more handsome than she'd remembered was a minor inconvenience. One she'd simply ignore.

"When do you start?" Maddie asked.

"Wednesday morning at nine." Erica could hardly wait to get her hands into finishing her very own tiny home. One with a little woodstove for those cold Wyoming nights. She'd get a lot of reading done in her downtime out there, something she already enjoyed. A shiver of loneliness skittered down her spine. She was used to that, too.

She imagined that she'd make some surface-level friends at each traveling assignment and be fine. Between commitments, maybe she could visit her daughters, both of whom lived in opposite directions. One in Colorado, the other in Florida.

"Well, it all sounds exciting. I've never been anywhere farther than Wisconsin. Bo promised to take me to Finland, but we haven't figured out when." Ruth crumpled up her cup and tossed it in the trash. "I better get the boys from outside and rescue Nora from saving our seats. See you inside."

"See you inside." Erica nodded.

Ruth had two young boys and a mother-in-law who meant the world to her. They had been the reason she'd remarried—to save her late husband's business. But Ruth had found love with Bo Harris, her new partner in work and life. Another second-chance blessing.

"I better go, too, and join the worship team." Maddie hurried into the sanctuary.

Leaving Erica alone to savor the last of her coffee.

Always alone.

She'd been an only child whose parents had died in a car accident soon after she'd married Bob Laine. He'd helped her through that loss. Having two baby girls, two years apart, soon after had lessened the sting, but there'd been no holidays spent at Grandma and Grandpa's house.

Bob had been a late-in-life child and his parents had been deceased long before she'd met him. His siblings were all quite a bit older, too, so there'd been no extended-family activities there, either, with the exception of a very dull reunion.

Only Ben had known her as a child and part of a thriving family.

Ben.

Why did seeing him again bring yearnings for family? Maybe it was simply because she was on the edge of leaving the only home she'd ever known. She'd wanted to leave the Upper Peninsula her whole life and now she was finally doing it. A little nostalgia was natural, and that was all it was.

Chapter Three

Wednesday morning, Erica arrived ten minutes before nine o'clock at the Fisher place. Ready to roll up her sleeves and get to work, she walked toward the large pole-barn workshop. Inside, she heard the sound of a saw. It stopped and then came a somewhat muffled discussion. Jason and Ben were working inside the larger tiny home and the vibe seemed tense. Something wasn't fitting right. There was no way she'd interrupt now, so she waited.

And waited.

Atlas walked over and sat by her feet, looking at her with forlorn eyes. Evidently, he'd picked up on that tension, too.

She scratched behind his ears. "You're a sweet boy."

"He's certainly that and more." Ben's mom walked toward her with a tray of what looked like coffee and muffins. "How are you, Erica?"

"Mrs. Fisher! Can I help you?" Erica hadn't seen Ben's mom since Bob's funeral. It had been very kind of her and her husband to attend.

"I'll just set this down. And, please, call me June. Would you like some coffee and a banana-oatmeal muffin?" Ben's mom looked great and, as usual, gave her a warm smile.

Erica never turned down coffee and those muffins looked delicious. "Yes, please."

"It's black. That's how the boys drink it." June poured her a cup.

"That's fine." Erica was used to black coffee. On occasion, usually around the holidays, she might add a flavored creamer.

June offered her a muffin on a red, white and blue napkin. "I understand you've purchased a tiny home."

"Yes. The small one out back." Erica took a bite and nearly melted. "These are delicious."

"Thank you."

"I'm going to help finish it, too," Erica added.

"I heard. I think that's great. Welcome to the fun house." Ben's mom pointed at the big one, where Ben and his son were inside working. "If they ever get this one done. The buyers are supposed to pick it up in two days."

"Something's not going right in there," Erica warned as June approached the open door of the tiny home.

Ben's mom ignored the warning and stuck her head inside. "Coffee break."

"In a minute." Ben's voice sounded strained.

Erica listened as Ben and his son discussed how to get the stove to fit without having to cut too much more of the cupboard. She ran her hand over Atlas's fur. He was still sitting at her feet.

"Attie's keeping you company, I see." June smiled at her.

"He's a wonderful dog."

"He was Ben's K-9 partner for eight years in Grand Rapids until they both retired."

"Really? Wow, that's cool." Erica had no idea that Ben had been in a K-9 unit. Impressive. His foreign-sounding commands suddenly made sense. She'd read somewhere that many police dogs were trained using the German language so criminals couldn't influence the dog.

"Ta-da," Jason said in triumph. "I told you it would work."

"That's why you're the boss."

Erica heard Ben's chuckle and relaxed. Whatever had gone wrong was now right. The men exited, and both had sawdust in their hair, looking even more like father and son.

"Muffins! Thanks, Grandma." Jason reached for one from the plate on the tray. Then he noticed Erica and raised his muffin in salute. "One of the perks you'll get working here. The food is great."

"Nice." Erica didn't expcct Ben's mom to feed her. She'd already packed a lunch that was in a cooler in her car.

"I'll be back for the tray later." June smiled, then turned and headed for the house.

Erica watched Ben. He hadn't yet said a word to her as he poured himself some coffee and grabbed the baked good, which he made quick work of polishing off.

"Dad, if you'd like to get started with Erica on wrapping her home, I can finish up here." Jason set his empty coffee cup on the tray. "She's staying with the original plans, so the window openings will be the same as already cut."

"Sounds good." Ben downed his coffee before turning to her. "Let's go."

Erica placed her half-empty cup on the tray and followed Ben through the workshop to her little home under the pavilion. She felt like an oversize shoe, ready to trip and look foolish.

He looked at her hands. “Do you have gloves?”

She pulled a pair from the back pocket of her jeans and slipped them on. “Sure do.”

“I’ll be right back.” Ben retraced his steps the way they’d come.

“Okay.” Erica looked around as she waited for Ben to return.

She spotted Atlas lying in the sun on the grass just beyond the pavilion. A shelving unit had been set up under the pavilion with all manner of tools and boxes of what must be nails and fasteners. Those shelves hadn’t been there when she’d toured this little shed on wheels last week.

“Here’s what we’re going to do.” Ben had come up behind her.

She jumped, ready to laugh at being startled, but Ben didn’t look amused. She turned her chuckle into a cough instead.

He held a roll of slick-looking white paper, although it wasn’t paper. “We’re going to wrap the exterior with this. It will serve as a moisture barrier and windbreak.”

Erica nodded, but she had no idea what to do.

Ben grabbed a box labeled *plastic cap nails* and handed it to her. “Hold these for now.”

She noticed that he wasn’t wearing gloves. He didn’t wear a wedding ring, either, but the indentation was there, if barely visible. Maybe he didn’t wear his ring while working, or his marital status had recently changed. That might explain why he was back in Pine. The probability that Ben was no longer married made her feel even more uneasy. She didn’t want any distractions to her plans to leave Pine and an unmarried Ben Fisher promised to be a tempting diversion. Just looking at him was enough trouble.

She watched Ben measure from the bottom of the wood up. He made a mark and repeated making marks along the entire side. Then he slipped the measuring tape into his construction belt.

"Here, if you'll hold the end of the house wrap."

Erica set down the box of nails, so she could use both hands.

"I'll need those nails."

"Do you have another one of those belts?" She smiled as she bent down and retrieved the box of nails with one hand.

"I don't." He didn't smile. He took the roll of house wrap from her and lined it up against the side of the tiny home. "If you'll hold this right here, I'll nail it in."

Erica did as asked, but her heart sank. There'd be no friendly chatter on this job site, at least not with Ben. He was either still mad at her, or at life in general. Either way, this was going to be a very long day.

The next day, Erica pulled into her regular parking spot and was met by Atlas, who circled her feet, begging for pets. "Hello, Attie."

The dog yipped in greeting and followed her into the shop.

Today, she was prepared for tiny-home work. She'd purchased her own construction belt from the hardware store in Pine so she'd have needed items at the ready. What those might be were yet to be discovered.

Yesterday, she and Ben had successfully wrapped her tiny home and had prepped the window holes for windows. Although her role had primarily been to hold things while Ben secured them, she still felt like they'd accomplished quite a bit. Until Jason needed Ben's help with the twenty-eight-footer, as they referred to it, and had sent Erica on her way after working only six hours.

Ben and Jason were in that same larger tiny home when she arrived, so she peeked her head inside the open door. They were wrestling with a full-size refrigerator, so she watched quietly while they shimmied it in place.

"Looks nice," Erica finally said.

Jason smiled. "I'm glad you're here. I definitely need a woman's opinion on the finish work. Do you mind helping us? The clients are picking this up tonight."

"Sure. Whatever you need." Erica climbed inside.

The space was much roomier than hers, but more than she needed. The walls and cupboards were all natural pine. Pretty.

"I think it's too much wood. Should we paint the cupboards? I'm thinking a light sage-green, like this." Jason handed her a paint swatch.

"Won't dry in time," Ben grumbled.

Erica looked closely at the interior. There was a lot of wood, but it was beautifully done. The cabinets were lovely knotty pine with a natural, glossy-looking stain. The appliances were all black, as was the countertop.

"Well, what do you think?" Jason looked impatient and even a little nervous.

"The buyers wanted wood," Ben said.

Jason nodded. "Yes, but it's too monochrome. I think they'll be sorry for it."

Erica looked at the paint swatch and then glanced at the entrance door, which looked like wood, but didn't match. "I think the cupboards are perfect, but maybe paint that door for a pop of color and a backsplash behind the sink echoing that sage green might be nice."

Jason grinned. "Yes! That's it. In fact, I have some tiles left from my own build. Come look."

Erica followed Jason out the door, into the workshop, where he did indeed have some shiny sage-green tiles, nearly a perfect match to the paint swatch. "Do you have enough?"

Jason nodded. "I think so."

Ben had joined them in the workshop.

"Dad, if you and Erica wouldn't mind applying the tiles, I'll run and get the paint for the door." He grabbed one of the tiles to take with him.

Ben lifted a box of tiles and a tub of grout. "Can you manage the other box?"

"Sure." Erica bent down and picked it up. It was heavier than she expected.

"Great. See you in a few." Jason jogged for his truck.

Erica followed Ben's rigidly straight back. Was he irritated with her suggestion? Seemed like he was always annoyed with her and even though they'd only worked together one day, she was already tired of it.

Ben set down both burdens on the counter, then turned. "I'll grab the tools."

She nearly ran into him and bobbled the box she was carrying.

He reached out and steadied it. "Easy. That's all we got."

Erica looked up into his face. He'd aged well. His jaw was still strong and shaded by yesterday's stubble, making him look ruggedly attractive. His hazel eyes got her in trouble, though, because once she gazed into them, she couldn't look away.

"Here." Ben took the box from her hands and set it on the counter.

Erica felt her face flame and looked away. What was with her…staring at him?

"This is really a one-person job."

Great, she'd made him uncomfortable and now he was kicking her out. "Anything I should do in the meantime?"

Ben pulled a tennis ball from his construction belt. "You could entertain Atlas."

"Sure." Erica took the ball and left, but she fumed.

Once outside, she checked her watch. There was no way she'd accept payment for playing with Attie. That wouldn't be fair to Jason. It wasn't fair to her, either. She was wasting time that could be spent on her tiny home… if only she knew what to do.

Atlas perked up from his sunny spot. Seeing the ball in her hand, he circled her feet and yipped until she threw it as far as she could.

After more than half an hour of playing fetch with Ben's dog, Erica was about to go inside and check Ben's progress when he suddenly appeared next to her. "Oh, hey."

"Thanks for throwing the ball. He needs the activity."

Erica handed over the tennis ball. "He's a great dog. Your mom said he was your partner. Were you always in a K-9 unit?"

This time Ben threw the ball and it landed much farther than her attempts. "Not always, no. Atlas was my second K-9. Judge, my first, was killed in the line of duty."

"I'm so sorry to hear that." Erica imagined losing a K-9 partner was harder than simply losing a pet. She wanted to ask what had happened, but Ben didn't appear to welcome any questions.

Ben's face was shuttered. "He was a good partner. Attie's a Belgian Malinois, and when the department got him, we connected right away."

"What did you do as a K-9 unit?" Erica loved watching Atlas run. He looked more like a puppy than a retired dog.

"Atlas came trained in explosive detection from a kennel in Holland. He excelled at detection, so I finished up his training in sniffing out drugs, as well. We covered some big events at Van Andel Arena."

"Wow, did he ever find any bombs?"

"One, but nothing at Van Andel." Ben didn't elaborate.

"So where did he find it?" Erica persisted.

Ben looked at her with grim eyes. "We were about to search a suspected drug house and Attie wouldn't let me get close. He kept pulling on my pant leg. Before it dawned on me what he was doing, the back of the house exploded. I owe him my life."

Erica shivered. She couldn't imagine dealing with that kind of danger on a daily basis. Had Ben stayed in Pine, or even in Marquette, would he have been safer? "Why did you leave the area? I thought you wanted to police a small town."

Ben looked at her and she realized her error too late. "Once you broke it off, what point was there in staying?"

She spotted Jason pulling in and relief filled her. Now was not the time to rehash their broken engagement. It was time to get back to work and far away from their past.

Glancing at Ben, she asked, "Can I see what you did with the tiles?"

Ben didn't want to talk to Erica. Talking led to getting to know one another again and then to liking each other. And that was where things would get sticky. He didn't want to *like* Erica and he sure didn't want to fall in love with her all over again. He'd be stupid to think that couldn't happen. Especially after taking that box of tiles from her. The way she'd looked at him was like the years had fallen away and it was just the two of them again.

It had always been the two of them…until it wasn't.

Ben tried to focus on what his son was saying. He'd purchased the paint and wanted him and Erica to paint the door while he added a few more tiles to finish off the whole length of the counter. He'd purchased an extra box that matched.

"Do you want the inside or outside?" Erica asked.

"What?"

"The door." Erica pointed. "Inside or outside?"

"Outside." That way he could toss the ball to Atlas.

Erica stood before him. "Brushes?"

"Yeah. Follow me." Ben exited to the workshop, where all the painting gear was shelved. "Take your pick."

Erica chose two.

"Do you regret staying in Pine?" He hadn't meant for his voice to come out like a whisper, but it was something he'd always wondered. He quickly handed her a container for paint and grabbed one for himself.

Erica's big brown eyes widened, as if she'd been surprised at the question. Or maybe it was the soft way he'd asked. "No, not really. It was a great place to raise my two daughters and it's an easy commute to the hospital."

He mentally kicked himself for asking. He didn't want to know about her personal life. She had two daughters. He wondered what they thought of their mom living in a tiny home while she was a traveling nurse.

"I really look forward to seeing what I've missed, though, starting with Wyoming this September."

Ben tried to smile but failed. "Got the travel bug, have you?"

Her eyes clouded over. "Too many memories here."

Robert Laine's death. He was a jerk to think only of *his* pain. "I'm sorry about your husband."

"I know. I got your card. Thank you."

Ben nodded. Time to shut down the talking. "Let's get painting."

"Deal."

Of all the cards she must have received, she'd remembered his and it floored him. But then, they had shared so much growing up. They'd been friends a long time before their relationship developed into something more. She'd been a part of who he was and always would be.

By the time they finished painting the door and wiping off the dried grout of the tile backsplash, Ben had to admit that Erica had been right about the color placement. It made the space look pulled together.

"The color looks really nice," Ben said. "Especially the tile."

"It does." Erica had a smidge of paint on her nose.

"You have paint right here." Ben touched his nose. He wasn't about to touch hers. Touching her would be dangerous.

"Oh." Erica pulled up the neck of her T-shirt to scrub it off. "Is this your largest project?"

Ben nodded. "Yeah. The costliest one, too. Jason's a little nervous. He wants everything to be just right. The buyers are a couple whose parents are big deals in Marquette. Word of mouth from this one could be huge for him."

Erica smiled. "I'm sure they'll love it."

"We'll see."

Jason popped his head inside, careful not to touch the drying door that had been left open for better air circulation. "I've got an appointment with some folks who are looking. If you want to break for lunch, we can regroup after. Or, Dad, if you want to show Erica the windows that were originally ordered for her place." He focused his gaze on her. "We can order something different if you don't like them."

"Oh, I—" Erica began, then stopped.

Jason was already gone.

Ben chuckled. "Come on. I'll show you the windows, then we can eat."

"What happens if I don't like the windows?" Erica asked.

"I'm pretty sure we can return them." Ben led her to the back of the pole-barn workshop, where the other garage door was open. Against the wall were windows with grids. The casements were white, instead of the black they used in the twenty-eight-footer they'd just finished.

"Oh, why wouldn't I like these?" Erica smiled.

Why indeed? She hadn't complained once yesterday or today and they hadn't given her house much attention. He really should cut her some slack. She wanted her tiny home completed on time and he wasn't about to mess that up for her. The sooner her place was finished, the sooner she'd be out of his hair.

"Some people are fussy," he finally said.

Lori had been fussy about a lot of things—the house, her clothes, even the type of car she drove. He used to tease her about that, but she didn't like it. In hindsight, he'd done too much that she hadn't liked. Not sharing his feelings had ranked number one. But he couldn't. If he'd unpacked what he'd buried deep, he'd have been no good to anyone. Especially on the job.

Erica shrugged. "I'm not usually, but there's some things I put my foot down on."

Ben chuckled. "What's that?"

"I like my hot food hot, and cold food cold."

"That's it?" He didn't remember that about her. Maybe it was something she'd developed while married to the uppity Dr. Laine.

"That's it. What about you?"

"What about me?" Ben really needed to put the brakes on their chitchat.

"What are you fussy about? You seem to have a bit of a chip on your shoulder."

"I do?"

Erica nodded. "Is it a cop thing?"

"Maybe." Or maybe it was women who'd left him that made him edgy. "So we can either break for lunch now, or start work on your place."

Erica looked at her watch, then at him. "Can we eat? I'm really hungry."

"Sure. There's a picnic table on my parents' back deck. That's where we usually break for lunch." To make the distance shorter for his mom, who insisted on waiting on them.

"Okay. I'll grab my cooler and meet you there."

Great. He'd just invited her to eat with him. Yesterday, she'd eaten inside her car while she'd checked her phone. He watched Erica until he heard Atlas whine.

Ben grabbed the ball and threw it for him. How long could he keep this up with Attie? Throwing the ball wasn't the same as having a real purpose. Neither was building tiny homes…or was it? He wasn't quite sure about that yet. He actually liked the work, and he loved working with his son. Maybe his place was here.

It didn't take Erica long to catch up to him.

"Can I ask you something, Ben?"

He wanted to say no. It'd be safer to say no. "Sure."

"I noticed you're not wearing your wedding ring. Are you still married?"

Why?

He didn't ask, because he really didn't want to know why she wanted to know. "I'm recently divorced."

"Oh. I'm sorry." Erica looked sorry.

"Yeah, me, too." Ben walked to his parents' deck, where his mom met them with a tray of sandwiches, chips and lemonade.

He was grateful that his parents joined them for lunch because he'd just closed down the conversation highway. He knew it was dangerous to talk to Erica. She'd always been good at getting him to open up and tell her things he didn't share with anyone else. He wasn't falling into that trap again.

He'd seen the question hovering in her eyes when he'd told her his first K-9 had been killed. He didn't want to break down into a blubbering idiot by explaining how Judge had died. And he sure didn't want to admit to how he'd responded.

The sooner they got this project done and over, the better. Erica Laine could then be on her way to Wyoming and he'd be glad to see her go. Really, he would.

Chapter Four

The following week, Erica chose a pair of shorts and a light T-shirt to wear to work on her tiny home. The weather forecast was for uncommonly hot temperatures, followed by more heat for the next couple of days. Which meant both days in the Fishers' pole barn and under the pavilion would be sweltering. The sun already felt scorching from a clear blue sky at eight o'clock in the morning; she could just imagine how oppressive it might feel this afternoon.

After pulling her hair into a ponytail, Erica slipped on a ball cap and headed for the kitchen to pack a sandwich and extra bottles of water. The spring in her step had everything to do with seeing what progress Ben and Jason had accomplished on her tiny home in the past five days, since she was last there. It had nothing to do with seeing Ben.

Yeah, right.

Why was there still this draw toward him? He had a hard shell that seemed to have formed around him. She didn't remember Ben being quite so guarded before. He didn't trust her as far as he could throw her.

With her cooler packed, she pulled on her socks and work boots and looked around, feeling a knot of tension between her shoulders tighten. She had boxes stacked in the corners that were partially filled with kitchen items she wanted to keep. She'd separated three corners into items for her tiny home, things for storage and donations. Erica had given in to the fact that she'd need to store some of her things. There were special dishes and keepsakes her daughters might want, along with stuff she didn't want to part with just yet, like some furniture from her parents.

"So much to do." Erica grabbed her cooler and headed out the door.

Telling herself that she had plenty of time to finish packing between her three twelve-hour shifts at the hospital and two days working on her tiny home, she slipped behind the wheel of her car, a six-year-old Subaru Outback that needed to be sold.

Erica had hung a For Sale sign on the back window, but so far, no calls. She'd left messages for a couple of dealers, too, but they hadn't gotten back to her. Time was ticking. The closing on her house had been bumped up to tomorrow because of the sellers leaving town or some such reason. She needed those thirty-five days until she left on August twenty-fifth, and had to push to make sure she got them. The bottom line was that her tiny house had to get done in time for her to get it ready to leave.

The drive to the Fishers' didn't take long since she lived only three miles away. She could walk there if she wanted to, but that might be tough with a cooler to carry. Not to mention the heat.

Erica pulled into the drive and parked, then spotted Jason and Ben in the pole barn. Country music poured from a radio as both of the huge garage doors were open, like always. The two men were standing near a trailer. They had a tripod set up at one end with something on top that Jason looked through, but Erica wasn't sure why. Ben stood holding what looked like a metal yard stick at the other end.

Once she got out of her car, Atlas came toward her at a run, whined and circled her feet.

It made both Ben and Jason look up and watch.

After petting Atlas, she walked into the shop, which was already a little stuffy. "Good morning."

"Morning, Erica." Jason waved. "Atlas acts like you're his long lost friend."

"Maybe I am." Erica loved dogs, but with her long day schedule, she couldn't have one.

Ben only tipped his head in greeting.

"What are you doing?"

"Making sure the trailer is level before we put up the walls on our newest order. It'll take us a few minutes before we're ready for you, so take your time settling in."

"Okay." She headed for the pavilion and her tiny home, thinking the whole way that construction was far more complicated than she'd originally thought.

Bracing herself for disappointment, she was pleased to see that the windows had been installed. That was about all that had been done, but it was something. She stepped inside, loving the light that poured in from those not-too-tiny windows.

She walked through the small space, envisioning where she'd put her things. Fingers of doubt inched their way into her chest and clutched at her heart. Was leaving everything she'd ever known the right thing? She'd been so sure that it was.

She heard someone approaching and turned.

"If you'll give us a hand with the framing this morning, this afternoon will be spent here." Ben had peeked his head inside the door she'd left open.

"Sure. The windows look great."

"We were able to get them in yesterday." His eyes locked on to hers. "It's going to be hot and humid today, so be sure you drink a lot of water and take breaks when needed."

Erica tipped her head. "I'm a nurse, remember?"

"Who works inside an icebox of a hospital."

"Very funny." He didn't miss a beat, did he? But it was true. She wasn't used to working outside in the heat. "I'll be careful."

He nodded. "That's all I'm saying. Since you're with us for a couple of days a week, I take it you work three twelve-hour shifts?"

"Every Monday, Tuesday and Saturday."

"Long days."

She spotted a flash of something close to admiration in his eyes. "Yes, but after all these years, I'm used to it."

She followed Ben back to the workshop. He'd not only talked a little more than usual, but he was also looking out for her. And it wasn't even starting time yet. Maybe Ben was softening. Erica nearly laughed. Instructions could not really be considered friendly conversation and his comments were not exactly soft.

Last week when she was here, after he'd admitted to a recent divorce, Ben had pretty much clammed up. She'd had to carry most of the conversation with his parents during lunchtime. Fortunately, they were kind people and it wasn't too awkward, but even they seemed to have sensed a shift in their son's mood. June had tried to get

Ben talking, but to no avail. Erica wasn't sorry for getting reacquainted with Ben's parents. She'd always loved them, too.

Once inside the pole barn, Jason gave more directions. "Here's what I need you to do, Erica. If you'll staple the sill seal along the edge of the trailer floor, like so."

Erica watched his demonstration and figured that was easy enough. She reached out to take the staple gun, but Jason was still explaining.

"Then my dad and I will attach the first row of plywood onto the wall and you'll help us lift it into place along the chalk line there, and then I'll secure the wall to the foundation."

"Got it." Erica pulled on her gloves and started stapling the roll of pink foam where Jason had shown her.

When that was done on all four sides, she helped lift the wall. It was hard work, and it was no wonder Ben had warned her about staying hydrated. She held one end opposite of Ben while Jason attached the wall to the trailer. And then Ben and Jason braced the wall with long boards and nailed it secure.

It suddenly clicked what Jason had explained about the process when she'd first looked at her tiny home—all of the frame pieces were premeasured and cut according to plans to make it go faster. Did it? She could only wonder.

When they got to the opposite long wall, Jason stepped back. "This will be tough, because we have to lift it up to clear the wall we just braced. Erica, grab the middle and watch out for the wheel well. Ready and on one, two, three—lift."

Erica was in the middle on the outside, while Ben and Jason lifted either end up from inside. She put her legs into it, but the wall wobbled and bam! As it dropped into place, her thumb got pinched between the wheel well and the framed wood.

She sucked in a breath as she pulled her hand away but her glove stayed put.

"You okay?" Jason asked.

For a moment, Erica couldn't speak, but she nodded. Her thumb throbbed—from the base to the end. Her skin had turned red with a bruise already starting. Breathing deeply, she walked to the opposite end of the wall from Ben to help steady it while Jason secured the bottom.

"Where's your glove?" Ben barked.

"Got stuck," she muttered. She kept breathing deeply, in and then out, until the pain subsided somewhat.

Jason made quick work of attaching the wall to the floor. "I need some ice," Erica announced while the men braced the opposite wall. She didn't wait for a response and ran to her car, grabbed the cooler and took out an ice pack, which she placed on her swollen thumb.

"That's why you don't hire a client!" She'd overheard Ben grumble the words at his son as she walked back into the workshop in time to see Ben pull her glove out from under the wall. The thumb section tore off, forever stuck between the wall and wheel well of someone's tiny home. It would have made her laugh if her thumb didn't hurt so much.

Both Ben and Jason bore down on her.

"Let me see." Ben was first to her side.

"It's fine. Not broken, just bruised." Erica didn't want to show him. She didn't want to cause a fuss, especially since Ben had already scolded his son.

"Erica, I'm so sorry." Jason looked more than sheepish.

"Please, it's no big deal," Erica assured him. "It could have happened to anyone."

"Let's take a break," Ben said.

The problem was that it didn't happen to anyone. It had happened to her because she hadn't been quick enough. She really needed to be more careful. She needed to be mindful of more than just the physical aspect of this side job. She'd made a commitment to the hospital in Wyoming. They were counting on her to fill in and she couldn't let anything or anyone jeopardize her fulfilling that agreement.

Ben didn't like Erica's brave front. He knew by her tight expression that she was in pain, yet she still refused to show him her thumb. He grabbed the first-aid kit and walked over to where she was sitting on a shop stool. "Let me see."

She looked at him with irritation but finally removed the ice pack and held out her hand. Her thumb was swollen and a nasty-looking reddish purple bruise appeared along the fleshy part of her palm at the base of her thumb.

"Can you move it?" he asked.

She wiggled it. "See, it's not broken."

"You'll be useless today." How was she supposed to help out now?

"I will not. It's only my left thumb. I'm right-handed. Do you have any gauze in there? I'll just wrap it up for a little extra cushion and get back to work."

"I'll do it. Give me your hand." Ben didn't mean to sound like an ogre, but she'd scared him. She could have been seriously hurt, and then what…? He'd have that guilt to carry around, not to mention that Jason's worker's comp insurance would go sky-high.

Erica complied by holding out her left hand. She still

wore her wedding ring—a wide gold band with a nice-size diamond in the center.

Gently, he wrapped the gauze around her thumb and then around her wrist to secure it. Holding on ever so lightly, he asked, "Not too tight?"

"No. It's good." Her voice sounded hoarse.

He met her eyes and couldn't look away. Too late, he realized he was still holding her wrist.

"Iced coffee?" His mom arrived with a loaded tray. "Erica, dear, what happened?"

Ben let go of her and reached for the carafe of regular brew. He still drank his coffee hot, no matter what the outside temperature.

"I pinched my thumb."

Ben shook his head at that fib, considering her glove now had a thumb hole. She could have smashed her entire hand.

Jason reached for a cookie. "Thanks, Grandma."

"I also brought a thermos of ice water."

"Thanks, Mom." Ben grabbed a cookie.

He was relieved to see that Erica downed an entire bottle of water from her cooler. He followed Jason into the little office. Keeping his voice even, he said, "We have to be careful with her."

Jason held up his hand. "I know, I know."

"You don't. She doesn't know what to expect on a work site, so we're going to have to warn her of possible dangers and make sure she's ready for them."

"Right." Jason let out a defeated breath. "You're right. She's pretty strong, though. She lifted with her legs instead of her back, like a pro."

Ben had noticed that, too. Although he and Jason had shouldered the heaviest load on either end, Erica had supported the wall while they had angled it up over the wheel well.

Erica stood in the doorway. "Okay, what's next?"

Ben had to give her credit for not giving up. She had her gloves back on, her wrapped left thumb sticking out like the sore thumb it had to be. Feeling the corners of his mouth twitch, he said, "The other two walls."

"Let's go."

What was her hurry? But, checking his watch, he noticed it was nearing eleven o'clock. They broke for lunch at noon and she'd want to get cracking on her place. Which meant he'd be the one working with her, but not until they'd finished sheathing the walls with plywood. Jason would need both of their help with that and her tiny home would have to wait.

By the time they broke for lunch, Ben was hot and sweaty. The walls were up and the plywood had been hung on one of the long walls, as well. He threw the ball for Atlas and glanced at Erica. "How's the thumb?"

"Sore."

"You can take off for the day now, if you'd like."

She shook her head. "Nope. I'm skipping out early tomorrow for my closing, so I'd like to get as much done today as I can."

Ben felt his eyes go wide. "Closing? You sold your house?"

"I did."

"When do you have to be out?" If Ben had any doubts, hearing that Erica had sold her house clearly proved she was leaving for good.

"The morning of August twenty-fifth. But I hope to be hauling that tiny home to Wyoming sooner than that.

My eldest daughter lives sort of on the way in Boulder, Colorado."

About a month away. No wonder she was antsy to get her tiny home completed. "How long did you live there, in the house you sold?"

Erica scrunched her face. "Ever since Bob and I were married. It was his house."

"Oh." Ben shifted as Atlas returned with the ball.

This time, he dropped it at Erica's feet.

Ben watched in amusement as his K-9 partner yipped and circled Erica instead of him. "He wants you to throw it."

"You think?" She gave him a smart look, then picked up the ball and tossed it. "I don't know why. I can't throw it nearly as far as you."

Ben shrugged. He wasn't sure, either. For some reason, Attie had taken to Erica from the moment they'd met. And Atlas was a good judge of character. The best, in fact. The dog had a sense about people that was downright uncanny. So what was this fixation with Erica all about?

They made their way to his parents' picnic table, where Jason was already seated. The canopy gave them shade, but it was still hot. Much too hot for a normal summer day in the Upper Peninsula of Michigan.

Erica had her little cooler in hand. Out of it, she pulled a measly-looking sandwich. No wonder she was so thin.

"I'm going to wash my hands. Erica?"

"Yes, please." She followed him inside. At the kitchen sink, she unwrapped her left hand and her thumb was purple along the base.

"That looks horrible."

Erica shrugged as she soaped up and then rinsed. "It could have been worse."

"That's what bothers me."

She turned on him. "You don't think I have what it takes for this kind of work, do you?"

"I never said that."

"You don't have to. I see it in your eyes every day." She wiped her hands and left.

Ben shared a look with his mom, who had overheard them.

"She's trying, honey. No doubt, she has a lot riding on this tiny-home purchase."

Ben didn't need to be reminded of that. Erica had chosen Jason to provide her living accommodations for her time spent as a traveling nurse. Her tiny home needed to be safe and road-ready as soon as possible. He didn't want to mess that up, but he didn't want Erica getting hurt, either.

He didn't want to get hurt himself and caring about her was a straight flight to just that. He really needed to forget their past relationship and treat her like any other customer or any other coworker. No matter how hard that might be.

Seated on the back deck, Erica relaxed for a moment, grateful the ibuprofen she'd taken when she'd grabbed her lunch cooler was kicking in. Between the heat and the throbbing of her thumb, she felt cross. She'd sounded it, too. She owed Ben an apology, but something about the way he watched her, as if expecting her to screw up, got under her skin.

He did, too. She cared about what had happened to him—why the divorce, why the retirement? None of which was her business, not to mention she was leaving Pine for good. She had no business getting involved in the *whys* of Ben Fisher.

Her plans had looked good on paper, and she'd wanted to travel for as long as she could remember. Bob had taken her on some exciting vacations, but they'd been quick weeks snatched here and there over the years. Now that she was finally acting on her plan to leave Pine, doubts bloomed like weeds popping up where she didn't want them. Maybe she should have simply rented a temporary apartment until she was used to being a traveling nurse. That might have been smarter.

"What do your daughters think about you selling your house?" Ben asked, then sipped some lemonade.

His mom had made a large, ice-filled pitcher and Erica finished her second glass, surprised at the personal question. "They're not thrilled. Their biggest concern was not having Christmas in the house where they grew up. Since I don't know where I'll be in December, the holidays are up in the air for me."

Ben's expression soured. "You've got time to decide, I suppose."

What had she said wrong now?

She did have time, but the days were passing fast and she still had loose ends to tie up, including the completion of her tiny home. "Are we finishing up the plywood?"

"Yeah, but it should go pretty fast and then we can work on your place. We need to tape the house wrap seams, then paint or stain the siding depending on what you choose."

Erica smiled as she stood, excited to finally get working on her project. "I'm ready."

Ben glanced at his son. "Jason, we ready?"

"Yup." He downed the rest of his lemonade and stood.

"Thanks for lunch, Mom." Ben kissed his mother's forehead. It was a sweet gesture.

"Yes, thank you, June. You make the best lemonade."

"Don't bring your lunch tomorrow, Erica, and I'll make something fun." Ben's mom winked at her.

Jason grinned. "See, a great perk."

"I look forward to it," Erica said. To do otherwise would be rude. And June's sandwiches looked far better than her slapped-together turkey with lettuce and mayo.

With her thumb rewrapped, compliments of Ben, they entered the sweltering workshop. Someone had turned off the radio, but the constant hum of a large fan in the far corner filled the space with white noise. The fan moved the hot air around, but didn't give much relief. Erica could feel sweat trickle down her back and she was standing still.

"Let's finish this up, then call it a day," Jason said. "We can start extra early tomorrow morning while it's cooler."

Erica wanted to protest, but didn't. It was hot, nearly ninety degrees, and Jason was the boss.

"We can still tape those seams." Ben's deep voice was low as he leaned close. It was as if he conspired against the early quitting time.

"We'll see."

She wasn't sure what she wanted to do, but two and a half hours later, Erica was spent. Hanging the plywood took longer than expected, but they got it done.

"I think we should go for a swim," Jason announced.

"Where?" Erica considered the oversize pond on the walking trail. It didn't look deep enough to swim in, but they could at least cool off. Might be a little mucky, though.

Ben gave her a surprised look. "What about taping?"

Erica shrugged. She was hot, tired and her thumb hurt.

"I know the perfect place." Jason winked. "Dad, grab a couple of towels and I'll take my truck."

Ben looked at her again. "I'm game if you are."

"Why not?" Erica had a million things to do, but the temptation of cooling off took precedence. She looked around for Atlas. "What about Attie?"

"He's in the house enjoying the air-conditioning with Millie."

"Millie?"

"My parents' dog. She's old and doesn't move around much. I'll be right back with towels."

Erica hadn't seen Millie when she was inside washing her hands. Odd. She watched Ben jog across the yard. Was this swim a good idea? It sure sounded good. Nothing waited for her at home but boxes and sorting. Not something she enjoyed. With every item she considered keeping came the memories.

"We'll put in extra time tomorrow on your place," Jason said.

"Thank you." Erica slid into the back seat of Jason's crew cab truck before she changed her mind.

He was going with them, so it wasn't like she'd be alone with Ben. The last time they'd gone swimming together, they'd been engaged. They'd gone to Black Rocks in Marquette— Panic squeezed her heart. Surely, they weren't going there. "How far is this place?"

Jason grinned as he climbed in behind the wheel. "Not far. Just a short drive. You'll see."

Ben climbed into the passenger seat and handed her a towel.

Erica wracked her brain to think of a swimming spot

close by. She glanced at Ben. He knew where they were going—she could tell by the smile that hovered at the corners of his mouth. "Okay, where are we going?"

"The river," he said.

Erica could have kicked herself. Of course. She and Ben used to go there when they were kids. Teenagers. The Pine River was where they'd shared a first kiss. She glanced at Ben again. Did he remember? He must have. But was he thinking about it? Surely not. That was a long time ago. Another lifetime, it seemed.

They pulled onto a two-track road that ended at a wide spot near the Pine River. Ben hopped out of the truck before Erica could get a read on what might be going on in his thoughts. It was probably better not to know.

She got out, took off her boots and socks and placed them back in the truck. The sandy expanse of bank led to a wide curve in the river, where the bottom was also sandy. She'd floated on inner tubes in this river with her girls and even once with Bob. There was a livery farther up that rented tubes and rafts. Bob had never been a big fan of floating, complaining that it took too much time with nothing else to do but float. He'd missed the whole point.

Erica smiled as she watched Jason and Ben strip off their T-shirts, run right into the water and dive in without testing it first. It would be chilly, but on a hot day like today, no doubt glorious.

Ben stood up with a gasp. "Whoa, that's cold."

"You get used to it." Jason dove back under.

Erica gingerly made her way to the water's edge, wiggling her toes in the wet sand beneath the surface. "It is chilly."

"You always did test the water first," Ben said.

He remembered.

Of course, he would, but Erica was still thrown off-kilter by the contemplative look in his eyes. Was he remembering more? The view of him standing in the water, waiting for her like when they were kids, took her way back. Ben had matured, sure, and so had she, but being here with him now felt the same as it did then. Exhilarating.

He walked toward her, holding out his hand in a coaxing manner. "Come on in, it's not bad. Not once you're in."

Erica refused to take it. She was struggling with memories of the two of them and taking his hand would only make her long for what might have been. In an uncharacteristic move, she darted to the right and dove under. The water was indeed cold, but in contrast to the sticky heat of the day, this was exactly what she needed. She came up to the surface, flipped over and floated in the gentle current on her back.

Sunlight shone through the tree leaves above. Tree growth was sparser at this point on the river, but there were a few old oaks standing guard along the shore. She couldn't believe no one else was here, but then it was nearly four in the afternoon. Not exactly prime sunbathing time.

Erica kicked her feet, hearing Ben and his son splash around behind her. She'd left the tension of the day on shore and enjoyed this quiet moment. Until she heard Jason's Tarzan-sounding bellow and looked up. He'd climbed one of the trees that hung over the deepest part of the bend and jumped. Ben followed suit. The two carried on like a couple of kids and it made her smile.

Ben had a strong relationship with his son. It was obvious that they were close and a twinge of envy twisted in her belly. She wasn't nearly as close to her daughters as she used to be. Once Ashley, and then Emily, had gone away to college, it felt like the strings that attached them had been cut.

Erica turned over and swam against the current, back to where she'd stepped into the river. She felt like her life had become a similar exercise. The harder she swam, the more the current seemed to take her downstream, bombarding her with memories of what had been hers but now was gone. She hoped the traveling-nurse assignment proved to be easier waters. Or at least happy swimming.

Chapter Five

Ben got out of the river and grabbed his towel. He glanced at Erica, who was sitting on a thick tree branch hanging over the edge of the river, dangling her bare feet in the crystal-clear water. She had bright pink polish on her toes that screamed *summer at the beach.* From the look of her golden skin, he'd guess that she frequented the sandy beaches located less than an hour's drive both north and south of them.

Wrapped in her towel, she looked lost in thought. Did she remember that this was the very place he'd first kissed her? The summer she turned sixteen, they'd ridden their bikes here to cool off, like they'd always done, but he'd changed everything between them that day with a single kiss.

Thinking about it, he could almost taste the peppermint bark they'd eaten just before. They'd both been drenched from swimming and yet she'd been so warm, her skin hot, like she'd been sitting near a campfire. They'd been just kids, and yet he'd known she was the one for him. He'd always known that he'd marry her one day, but it never happened.

Erica caught his gaze and smiled. She looked much like she did then, with her hair wet and slicked back on a hot summer day similar to this one so many years ago. A lifetime ago.

"Ready to go?" he called out. He'd had enough of memory lane.

"Yes." She hopped off the branch into shallow water and trudged toward him. "This was great."

"Yeah."

"Remember when we used to come here?" Her brown eyes looked wistful and sweet.

"Yeah." He remembered.

Recollections he hadn't thought about in years leaked into his mind, churning up bittersweet memories. Those same remembrances twisted into mockery, taunting him with everything he'd done wrong. He'd lost Erica and he'd lost Lori. The emptiness inside him only grew.

"And what did you two do here?" Jason wiggled his eyebrows.

Ben wasn't going there, so he swung his towel to twist it and snapped his son's thigh.

"Owww!"

Erica laughed.

She didn't seem bothered by their past. To her, they were probably just fond childhood remembrances. To him, they still bordered on painful.

"A bunch of us kids used to ride our bikes here and swim. When we could drive, we still came here," she said. "It's been a long while since I was last here with my daughters."

"Nice." Jason nodded. "Molly and I found this place that last summer we stayed with Grandma and Gramps. Remember, Dad? I was, like, fifteen."

"I remember." Ben used to take Lori somewhere special for their own little vacation when the kids were at his parents' place.

At first, it had worked out great. But as the kids got older, they didn't stay as long and Ben's work schedule grew more demanding as he went up the ranks. The fact that he'd grown distant from his wife didn't make things any easier.

Jason turned to Erica as they walked toward the truck. "I loved it here, but Molly didn't want to leave her friends downstate. I came up on my own after that."

"Pine is a nice place," Erica agreed as she climbed in the back seat.

Yet, she wanted to leave.

The ride back to the workshop was quick and quiet. When Ben peeked in the back seat, Erica had her head tilted back and her eyes were closed. She was cradling her left hand with her right and the purpling bruise at the base of her thumb had darkened.

He gritted his teeth as he exited the truck.

"Thanks for the swim. I'll see you both tomorrow. What time are you starting?" Erica grabbed her boots and socks, but didn't bother putting them on. Those hot pink-painted toes looked out of place against a dirt two-track.

"Pretty early," Jason said. "I'd like you to come by at your regular time, though."

Ben was glad of that. They'd probably get more done without worrying over her injury.

"Sounds good." Erica waved as she headed for her car with the For Sale sign hanging in the back window.

Ben watched her pull out. Jason had gone into his own tiny home, no doubt to relax and maybe even catch a nap before dinner.

His parents were spoiling both of them with wonderful lunches and dinners, but it brought his mom joy to fix them. He could tell she missed having family in the house. His dad, too. Jason rented the workshop from them, but Ben knew his parents would have offered it for free if it meant having family close by. Guilt seared his gut. He should have visited more. Looking back, he should have done a lot of things more.

He didn't bother changing out of his damp T-shirt and swim trunks. He headed for the pavilion and Erica's tiny home. He'd at least get the wrap seams taped and spray foam around the windows to seal them.

A few minutes later, Atlas came charging toward him.

Ben stopped and lavished attention on the dog. "Hey Attie."

"He knew you were out here." His mom offered him a tall tumbler of iced lemonade.

"Thanks. I should have come in, but I wanted to get this done before settling in for the night."

"It's a cute little thing."

Ben chuckled. "The tiny home?"

His mom nodded. "I've been telling Jason that you should name these models as you complete them. Makes it easier to refer to them by name rather than size."

"That's a good idea. What would you call this one?" Ben patted Erica's tiny home.

His mom tipped her head. *"The Wanderer."*

Ben raised his eyebrows in surprise. "Hey, that's good. Maybe we should get you in on marketing."

"Maybe so. Well, take your time. Dinner won't be for a bit yet."

"Thanks, Mom. For everything."

"You're my son. No thanks needed." She turned and walked back toward the house.

Ben looked at Atlas sitting at his feet as if waiting to see what he'd do next. A walk after dinner might be nice, but for now, he needed to get *The Wanderer* taped and the windows sealed.

It was a perfect name for an easy-to-haul tiny home. But even more so, it described Erica's goals. She wanted to wander. Once she got her fill of traveling, would she return? Or would she forever wander to escape the memories of losing her husband?

The following morning, Erica found Ben and Jason inside the workshop, framing the roof of the other tiny home. "Hi."

"Hey." Ben nodded.

"We're just about done with the frame. I'll be down in a minute to get you started on your place," Jason said.

Erica smiled, feeling more positive than she did yesterday. "Great! I'll head over there."

The weather forecast called for thunderstorms in the afternoon, but she doubted that would happen. The humidity wasn't as bad as yesterday, but then the sky looked overcast with haze in the distance. It was still warmer than normal, though. Seventy-five degrees at nine in the morning wasn't normal in the Upper Peninsula.

She stared at her little shed-on-wheels in awe. The wrap seams had been taped and plastic furring strips were attached to the outside. She also spotted yellow spray foam peeking out from under the windows.

"Who?" she whispered under her breath.

"My dad. He did all this last night."

Erica whipped around to see Jason standing with his hands on his hips. “He did? Why?”

“He needs to stay busy, otherwise he thinks too much. He also feels bad about your hand. How’s the thumb?”

Erica had iced it really well last night and the swelling was down. She extended her hand, palm out. “It’s good.”

Jason smiled. “I’m glad. I feel pretty bad about it, too.”

She waved away his concerns while her thoughts swirled. So Ben had worked on her tiny home after their swim. Not because he was being kind, but because he was plagued by his own thoughts. Was it his divorce, or something else? Did any of his thoughts include her?

“The siding is stacked along the back in the workshop. The original buyers chose gray paint, which I have. But if you want a different color, we can get it. I have several stain options, but honestly, that won’t last as long as the kind of paint we have.”

She’d rather not waste time picking out colors. “Can I see the gray paint?”

Jason smiled. “Sure. It’s in the workshop.”

She followed him and he showed her where to find the stacked lengths of pine siding. She inhaled the wood smell, then glanced at the other tiny home, while Jason worked on opening the lid to the paint can. Ben, dressed in shorts and a T-shirt, was standing on the tippy top of the roof with a nail gun, securing the sheathing. The whooshing sound, followed by a corresponding snap, filled the air, but her gaze was fixed on the man making the noise. Ben looked so strong and sure, but hard, too, like he’d seen too much in his life. No doubt, as a police officer, he’d seen more than most. Was that what plagued him?

“Here it is.” Jason held the open can.

Erica focused back on the paint. The light shade of gray looked creamy. Pretty, even. "I'll use it. It's nice."

"Great." Jason helped her set up several lengths of siding on sawhorses under the pavilion. He instructed her to paint both sides.

She got to work, humming as she covered the pine planks. She liked the color even more as she painted. With the white gridlines of her windows and white trim, her little shed-on-wheels would look very cottage-like when it was all done. Excitement at seeing it complete chased up and down her spine. She could hardly wait.

After some time, Ben joined her with a brush. "That color looks nice."

"I think so, too." Erica kept painting. She'd take a break soon to let the sides she'd painted dry, then flip and paint the others. Finally, she looked up. "Thank you for working on this last night."

He shrugged. "No big deal."

"It is to me." After a long pause, Erica said, "Jason said you need to keep busy. How come?"

"I'm not used to being retired."

Erica studied him a second or two. By the way his jaw worked, she knew that wasn't all of it. "And?"

"And hands-on work keeps my thoughts at bay," he finally added.

He seemed so closed, yet she'd spotted a glimpse of suffering. Had his divorce been painful or was that her imagination at work? Either way, she wanted to help. "Do you attend a church in the area?"

"Why?" he chuckled.

"Well, I wanted to know if you went anywhere before I invited you to attend my church."

"Why would I go to your church?" His voice dripped amused sarcasm.

"Why not go?"

He chuckled again. "Erica, have you become one of those Bible-thumpers?"

Slapping the paint on her last length of siding, Erica chuckled at his teasing. "Well, I don't make a practice of thumping anyone with the Bible, but I do believe in salvation through Christ. What do you believe in?"

"Not much." He looked at her with challenge in his eyes. "Other than Atlas and my family."

Ouch.

She gazed back without flinching. He was trying to unnerve her, but it wasn't going to work. She'd play his game, but she'd be honest, too. He needed God in his life. "Then I'm going to pray for you."

Surprise mingled with irritation in the depths of his hazel eyes. "You do that."

"I will."

Really, she should leave him alone and keep the conversation to construction work. They had a lot to do yet, and she was leaving early today for her closing appointment.

Erica balanced her brush across the paint can. "I'm going to take a water break while these dry. Would you like to join me?"

"Are you going to Bible-thump me?" The teasing gleam was back.

"You could probably use it, but no." Erica smiled, even though Ben's comment about keeping his mind occupied bothered her. A lot.

They'd been such good friends before they'd started dating. Could they be friends again? She'd like to think so, but then she was leaving soon. The reality of that sank in hard. She had a lot to do and really needed to stay on task. Stay focused. Which meant she should quit digging into Ben's personal life.

She had her own personal stuff to deal with, leaving all this behind her. She'd looked forward to traveling for a long time. She and Bob had made big plans before he had his stroke. They'd been so close to buying a travel trailer, something they could comfortably live in while they drove from place to place. She was a woman alone now. Could she still fulfill that dream all by herself in a tiny home she helped complete? Erica vowed she'd give it her all, and not only to chase a few dreams, but also to find a renewed sense of fulfillment that she'd lost.

Ben couldn't keep Erica's statement that she'd pray for him out of his thoughts. Over and over, he replayed their conversation, wondering what had brought her to invite him to church. What was it that she saw in him that made her think he needed to be *saved*?

They'd painted the trim white and most of it was dry, or dry enough to hang. Ben framed out around the wheel well and the corners before they started tacking the painted pine in place, starting from the bottom. He wanted to get as much secured as possible before the gathering storm clouds rolled in on them, or Erica left for her house closing—whichever one came first.

They worked together quietly. He wasn't in the mood to talk. He didn't need her prayers, or want them. God had allowed events— He stopped there. How could God fix him? And even if God could, shouldn't He have done something to keep Lori from leaving him? Or, better yet, keep his partners alive?

Erica measured the next length and called it out to him. They were two lengths above the wheel well now. They had enough painted siding to get halfway up on one side.

He made the cut with the chop saw, brought it over and set it in place. "Hold it right here."

Erica held it while he tapped the board in place and checked that it was level before he nailed it to the plastic furring strips.

He wasn't sure he even believed there was a God. His parents believed, and they'd invited him to their church services since he'd come home. He'd been there, done that, growing up, and the formality of religion wasn't for him. Besides, Ben didn't want to rely on anyone but himself and Atlas. He trusted Attie—he'd trusted his other partners, too, but trusting didn't come easy. Trusting in something with no proof of existence other than a feeling wasn't something that appealed to him. Feelings swayed a person's judgment. Good one moment, bad the next.

"Ben?" Erica waved her hand at him.

He shook out of his thoughts. "What?"

"Thought I'd lost you there."

"What makes you believe there's a God?" The question was out before he could stop it.

"A whole lot of little things and big things." She smiled, looking as if she was contemplating what she'd say next. "To name one, there was a patient I had at the hospital with a benign tumor that needed to be removed. She'd prayed, her family prayed, and when she went in for surgery, it was gone."

Ben sneered. "You can't be serious."

"I was there—I saw for myself." Erica shrugged. "That's what made me seek God. I started reading the

Bible, and the more I read, the more real God became to me."

"There's that Bible-thumping."

"Maybe Bible-pumping is a better term. There's life-blood in those pages."

"Hmm." He wasn't sure about that. He'd seen his share of blood and had caused some of it, too. Just then, the wind picked up. "Here comes that storm."

Erica looked around. "Will the siding be okay out here?"

"We should move these back into the workshop so they don't get blown around. I'll close up the tools. That sky doesn't look good."

Erica glanced toward the darkening northwest sky and her eyes widened with concern. "Yikes."

"Yeah." Ben closed the big toolboxes with a click and looked around. *The Wanderer* was buttoned up with the installed windows and door. The metal roof hadn't been put in place yet, which was why it was under a pavilion. Tarping it now would be a waste of time in this wind. It should be okay.

Ben helped Erica take the siding inside the workshop. He carried in the chop saw next and then closed the big garage door. Jason was already closing the other.

The wind roared, followed by the tinkling sound of hail hitting the pole-barn roof. A flash of lightning blazed through the windows, then a crash of thunder literally shook the ground.

They looked at each other.

"We should head indoors," Ben said. They didn't need to be inside a metal building right now, grounded or not.

When they opened the door, the hail and the wind were whipping across the yard. Ben reached for Erica's right hand. "Come on."

She slipped her hand into his and they darted for the house. But she stopped and pointed at his parents' backyard. "Wait, there's Millie and Attie."

"Follow Jason—I'll get the dogs." Quarter-sized hail pelted his skin and it stung.

Atlas circled his parents' dog, barking. Millie had lain down, as if too tired to move. Hail bounced off her body and face. The poor girl had her eyes closed. The pathetic sight ripped through him with the reality that Millie was fast approaching the end of her years. Ben could hear his mom frantically call Millie's name from the back deck.

"I got her," he yelled, but his words were taken by the wind.

Another flash of lightning, followed by rumbling thunder, had him picking up his pace. When he reached the golden retriever, he bent down and lifted her into his arms. He shielded her face as best he could from the hail that was quickly turning to rain. Sheets of it came down, drenching his T-shirt.

Millie groaned.

"It's okay, girl. I got you."

Atlas danced at his heels, ready to assist.

"Good job, Attie. Let's get inside."

When they finally slipped through the kitchen slider, all of them were soaked through. Ben gently put Millie on her feet, then steadied her as her old paws slipped on the bare floor. She looked ready to collapse. "Mom—"

His mother put her hand up to silence him. She had tears in her eyes as she choked out, "I know, honey. I know."

He watched his mom gently rub down her dog with a towel. His throat grew thick, hearing Millie's soft whine of pain.

Erica handed him a towel and approached Atlas with another. “Come here, Attie. I’ll help you get dry.”

Ben wiped his face, trying to clear away the sadness caused by his mom’s tender ministrations to Millie, along with the raindrops. The dog’s days were numbered and they both knew it.

He heard Attie’s yip and smiled. Atlas was acting the puppy when Erica tried to towel him off. Attie darted away, then grabbed the edge of the towel as if it were a pull-toy.

“Atlas, *sitz*,” Ben commanded. His mom wouldn’t want a wet dog running through the house and he didn’t want Atlas knocking Millie down before she could reach her memory-foam bed.

Atlas sat.

“Thank you.” Erica smiled as she rubbed down Atlas with the towel. The dog licked her face and she laughed, then kissed his head.

Ben couldn’t look away from them. Erica didn’t wear a stitch of makeup and her dark hair was damp and tousled, but her beauty hit him like a lightning bolt, sizzling its way through his veins as clearly as the flashes still skittered across the sky.

Not good.

He felt his mom’s hand on his back. “Thank you for getting Millie.”

“Of course.”

“I’m hoping to have this last summer with her, before, well, you know what I’m trying to say.” His mother’s voice had grown thick.

He slipped his arm around her. “Yeah, I do.”

Those he’d loved had left him one way or another—first Erica, then his best friend Jack, Judge and Lori. He had no business letting Erica get inside him once again. Maybe he needed her prayers after all. Prayers that he'd keep a safe distance. Prayers that he wouldn't get hurt all over again.

Chapter Six

Friday was a beautiful day with clear skies and low humidity, but Erica spent her morning going through household items not included in the sale of her house. She had to finish sorting what else to keep or toss, but needed a break. She'd texted Ruth and Maddie, asking if they might be available for lunch, and both had agreed.

Slipping inside their regular meeting place at the Pine Inn Café, Erica noticed that both Ruth and Maddie were already seated at their usual table in the back that had a window view of the gardens. Both women waved. She was going to miss these lunch meetings. She'd miss Ruth and Maddie, who'd been a bright spot in her dull life this past year.

"You're late," Ruth scolded, then grinned.

Erica fumbled with the straps of her purse as she tried to hang it over the back of her chair. She finally set it under the table and sat down. "I know. I'm sorry. I just dropped off a load of boxes into my storage shed. It took longer than expected."

"No worries—we haven't ordered yet," Maddie said.

"How's everything?" Ruth asked. "You seem stressed."

"Stressed, frustrated, scared. Take your pick." Erica took a long drink from the water glass in front of her.

"What's going on?"

"Yeah," Maddie added. "What scares you, Erica?"

"I'm nervous that my tiny home might not get done in time. Yesterday, we were rained out, and then I had the closing on my house. There's no backing out now." Not that she wanted to back out. More than ever, she wanted to escape.

Ruth touched Erica's left hand, turning it palm up to reveal the bruised base of her thumb. It had taken on an ugly greenish hue where it wasn't purple. "Wait, what happened here?"

"I pinched it between a wall frame and the metal wheel well."

"Ouch," Maddie said.

"Yeah. The work is a little harder than I thought it would be," Erica confessed.

Ruth nodded as if she understood. "I know the feeling."

"Plus, it's frustrating to constantly switch from my tiny home and the one ahead of mine." Erica thought about Ben helping her paint the siding. He'd shut down after she'd invited him to church, but she didn't want to mention him. Not really.

"What happens if it's not ready in time?"

Erica took another drink, but shrugged. "I don't know. The guys know my timeline and how important it is. It'll get done."

It had to.

"Is that really what you fear?" Maddie persisted. "Moving away is a big change."

"It is, but I've been looking forward to this for a long time." She also looked forward to seeing Ben every

Wednesday and Thursday mornings, and that scared her. Driving all the way to Wyoming with her tiny house in tow scared her. Having regrets over her decision to become a traveling nurse scared her, too, and all in that order.

Ruth narrowed her gaze. "So who are these *guys* you work with?"

Erica felt caught off guard by the question. Ruth was clearly digging; Maddie, too. They might be onto her that the completion of her tiny home was really the least of her worries.

When they used to attend the grief support group together at church, Pastor Parsons often said that fears needed to be vocalized in order to deal with them properly. Erica didn't want to whisper one word of her growing attraction for Ben. Saying it aloud seemed to make it more real and scary.

The tender way he'd carried in his parents' dog out of the rain—and then his sorrow-filled interaction with his mother—had touched her deeply. For such a gruff guy with a chip on his shoulder, he'd been pretty sensitive. Pretty awesome, too.

Erica took a deep breath. "Well, I work for this young man and his father works with him, too."

"Anyone we know?" Maddie asked.

Erica shook her head. Maybe she should just spill the beans. It might make her feel less anxious to finally fess up. "Not likely, but the father and I were once engaged, before I met Bob."

Ruth's golden-brown eyes glowed. "Wow. What a coincidence. Is he married?"

"Recently divorced."

Ruth and Maddie exchanged a look.

Erica shook her head. "Don't even go there. I'm leaving Pine for a very long time."

"But you're only contracted for thirteen weeks at a time," Ruth pointed out. "You could come back."

Erica didn't want to come back. At least, not permanently. She'd had enough of living in Pine, where reminders of Bob, and now Ben, were everywhere.

"Is he a good guy?" Maddie asked.

"Yes. But he's not a man of faith. Ben's a tight ball of hurt and anger." Some of it might be her, but Erica had the feeling there was something more than just his divorce that ate away at Ben's peace.

Ruth and Maddie exchanged another look between them. "What?"

"What if this is your second-chance blessing? God might have brought you two together for any number of reasons, but what if you need each other? You obviously loved him once—could you love him again?"

Erica laughed to cover how close to the truth that statement might be. She didn't want to fall in love with Ben all over again. Not now, not when she was leaving. Not when he didn't believe in God, like she did. Not when they were so different than they used to be.

When they were kids, they'd had so much to talk about and share. It was like they couldn't wait to be together. Sometimes they'd even finished each other's sentences. Now? She didn't know what went on inside of him. Before witnessing yesterday's moment with his mother and her dog, Erica had thought Ben cold. Unfeeling, even.

Maybe that's all a cover.

Erica didn't want to find out, but then again she did. And that made it all the more frustrating.

"Well?" Ruth pressed.

"No." Erica sighed. "I don't want to love him."

Ruth squeezed Erica's shoulder. "I know how you feel."

"Sometimes, it just happens." Maddie smiled.

"Not if I don't let it." Erica looked over the menu in order to shut down this conversation trail before she lost her footing.

She wasn't about to admit that she prayed for Ben that morning during her devotions. And she wouldn't acknowledge that Ben made her feel alive. Even if only because he'd rattled her. A lot.

"Well, at the very least you'll have an interesting last few weeks. If you need help packing, let me know," Ruth offered.

"Yeah, me, too," Maddie said.

"Thank you. So far, I'm still figuring out what I'll need to take and what I want to store." Erica knew she wouldn't ask for their help. Both Ruth and Maddie had young children to care for, not to mention businesses of their own to run.

The waitress came to take their orders and Erica listened while Ruth asked for her usual large salad plate and Maddie chose a club sandwich with fries. Erica went out on a limb and ordered a Denver omelet because she'd skipped breakfast.

And then she remembered that Ben's favorite meal had been a big breakfast. He used to make it for dinner when they were dating. Did he still do that? She needed to stop thinking about Ben. It wasn't good for her and they couldn't be good for each other after all this time had passed. They were two different people now.

Erica had had a comfortable marriage with Dr. Robert Laine. They'd loved and respected each other. Having worked together for years, they had practically agreed on everything. Erica had a hunch that Ben Fisher was anything but comfortable. Life with him would be a string of arguments and grumbles. So why did the very thought of him make her blood pump a little faster?

Wednesday and Thursday mornings were Ben's favorite of the week and he was sorry to admit that it was because of Erica. He looked forward to seeing her. This Wednesday morning, while Jason met with a couple of potential clients, Ben soaked in Erica's joy-filled reaction to the work completed on her tiny home. He and Jason had finished the siding, installed the metal roof and even put in a white coach light fixture near the door. The outside was done.

"Wow. This is so great," Erica said. "And where did you get this light? I love it."

Ben thought she would. "Jason had it. We can change it out if there's something you'd like better."

"No. No." Erica ran her fingers over it. "This is perfect."

"Good."

She turned to face him, her dark eyes shining. Again, she was wearing a simple T-shirt and shorts with her brown hair pulled up into a ponytail. She looked more like twenty-five than forty-nine. "Thank you."

Her genuine appreciation washed over him like a spring shower in the desert and he sucked it up as if parched. "You're welcome. We're getting close to you leaving, so now we can focus on the inside."

Erica nodded, but her smile drooped and her eyes dulled.

"What's wrong?"

"Nothing. It's just that it's getting real now."

Ben didn't want to care, didn't want to dig, either, but he did both, anyway. "Is this the first time you've moved away?"

She scrunched up her face. "Pretty obvious, huh?"

He chuckled. "Yeah, I suppose so, but that's okay. Can I ask why are you leaving?"

Erica's brown eyes sought his and didn't let go. "Did you ever lose sight of the purpose you once had?"

Had he ever. He'd gone to the police academy because he'd wanted to serve his community. He'd wanted to make a difference by enforcing the law and keeping people safe. He'd failed to keep his friend and partner, Jack, safe, and after transferring to the K-9 team, he hadn't kept Judge safe, either. "A couple times, yes."

"What did you do?" Erica leaned against a sawhorse. The warm summer breeze lifted the few strands of her hair that had come loose.

He resisted the urge to tuck those tendrils behind her ear. "I did what you're doing. Same job, only in a different area. I didn't move out of state, but I joined the K-9 team."

"Was it rewarding?"

"Very." Ben had been reenergized by working with dogs. His canine partners seemed to understand him more than most.

"Why did you retire? You're still young."

He let loose a bark of laughter. "I don't feel so young."

Just then, Jason came into the pavilion, followed by a young couple, his potential clients. "This is my dad, and Erica. And this is Erica's tiny-home-on-wheels, built to tow, if you'd like to view our smallest built home."

They all shook hands and the couple were eager to see the inside of *The Wanderer*, Erica's home.

Ben gestured for Erica to follow him into the workshop. "I think we have some staining to do."

As they grabbed supplies, Erica nudged him. "You never answered my question."

He wasn't sure how to answer. There was way too much tangled up in his reasons to quit the force. He might as well explain the basic reason. He couldn't talk about the other stuff. Not to her. Not to anyone.

Letting loose a sigh, Ben shrugged. "In the divorce, Lori got the house. Attie needed to retire and I didn't want to leave him alone all day in some apartment. I had my thirty years in, so I opted to retire with him and landed here, back home."

Erica's gaze narrowed. "When did this happen?"

"The divorce, or my retirement?"

"Both, I guess."

He ran his hand through his hair. "Beginning of June. For both."

"Wow, Ben. I'm really sorry." She touched his shoulder.

The warmth from her hand radiated through his whole arm, then his body, but it didn't quite reach his heart. He'd pulled back before that happened. Everyone was sorry—even Lori had been sorry—but sorry didn't do much for him. "Yeah. We might as well get to staining."

"Of course."

Erica helped him set up the heavy duty sawhorses and stack planks of pine siding on them. He poured a container of stain for each of them. They donned gloves, grabbed brushes and got to work. Staining went fast and neither of them spoke.

Ben appreciated the space Erica gave him, but part of him wanted to unload. She'd been a good listener in the past—his sounding board. What would she think if he told her everything? If he admitted to feelings a police officer was never supposed to have? The temptation to confess lingered on the tip of his tongue and stayed there. Ben was never more relieved as when Jason walked into the workshop.

His son slapped his hands together. “We have another sale.”

Erica looked up from her staining. “That’s wonderful.”

Ben knew better. “When’s our deadline?”

“Yeah, about that…” His son grinned. A surefire indication that the kid had overcommitted. “They’d like it by Labor Day.”

Ben felt Erica’s searing, wide-eyed gaze before he looked into her eyes. She was already worried about getting hers completed on time and here was another project that might be getting in the way.

“I told them I couldn’t guarantee it, but that I’d try. It depends on how fast we can get the interiors done on Erica’s and this one.” Jason knocked on the wrapped side of the twenty-footer.

“What did they order?” Ben asked.

“A small one like Erica’s.”

“Hmm, another one like *The Wanderer*.” Ben chuckled.

Erica gave him a quizzical look. “What do you mean?”

“My mom thinks we should name our tiny home plans, so they can be showcased and resold that way. She dubbed yours *The Wanderer*. It fits pretty well, don’t you think?”

She nodded but her expressive eyes had clouded over once again. Something was amiss. Should he find out what? It was none of his business, and the less he delved into what was bothering Erica Laine, the better. Because he might reciprocate with what was really bothering him. And that could be bad for both of them.

"Erica, would you like to stay for supper? I made barbecue ribs and there's plenty."

Erica glanced at Ben, but he was busy putting away tools and didn't look at her. Fine, if he wasn't going to give her any clue as to what he wanted, she'd choose what she wanted.

What she didn't want was to return to an empty house filled with boxes and try to figure out something to eat this late in the day. They'd worked a long one and it was nearing seven o'clock.

Giving Ben's mom a smile, Erica said, "Thank you, June. Barbecue ribs sound amazing and I'd love to stay. Is there anything I can do to help you?"

Ben stopped for only a split second. If surprised or bothered by her decision to stay, he didn't show it. He kept cleaning up the workshop area without a word.

His mother seemed to notice that brief hesitation, too, but she didn't point it out. Instead, she smiled back. "Actually, if you'd like to help me get a few things ready, I'd really appreciate it."

"Gladly." Erica glanced at Ben, but his back was turned, so she followed Ben's mom across the expansive yard into the farmhouse.

She'd always loved Ben's parents' house and the cozy atmosphere enveloped her like a warm hug. The Fishers' kitchen had always smelled of cinnamon and melted butter, and that hadn't changed. Erica felt like she'd just come home.

"It's such a nice night, I thought we'd eat out on the

deck. If you wouldn't mind wiping off the table." June handed her a roll of paper towels and disinfectant spray.

"I'd love to." Erica took them and stepped through the massive slider.

After wiping down the table, she scanned the grassy yard that included a flower bed and large vegetable garden. The back deck overlooked an expanse of lawn that led to the red barn. A smaller, matching version of a chicken coop stood next to the barn. A couple of rows of sunflowers tilted toward the afternoon sun just beyond. The wire fencing had a gate that was currently open so the chickens could range freely. There had to be at least a dozen of them roaming around, scratching and pecking at the ground.

Millie was lying in one of June's flower beds catching the evening sun. The dog watched as Attie milled around those chickens, trying to herd them back into their enclosure.

"He does this every evening." June held a tray of plastic plates, cups and silverware. She set it down. "I need to go help him get them inside the pen."

"I'll set the table," Erica said, but June was already down the deck steps and on her way to the chicken coop.

Erica smiled. June was still fit and active, as was Ben's dad, too. Ben was fortunate. His parents weren't going anywhere anytime soon.

"Well, hello, Erica." Ben's dad exited the house.

"Hi, Mr. Fisher."

"Please, call me Glen." He winked. "Staying for supper?"

"I am." She set the table.

"Good. You guys had a long day."

"We got a lot done." Erica had been impressed by just how much they'd tackled.

Her little cottage-on-wheels didn't look like a shed any longer. It had been moved from under the pavilion to make room for the twenty-footer. The workshop was ready for the new build order, which would be like hers. They'd already leveled the sixteen-foot trailer base in preparation for the subflooring and then the walls.

She could hardly wait to work on the inside of her place. She considered whitewashing the natural pine walls inside. Since it was so small, she wanted everything light and airy. She'd have to pick up some pretty plastic dishes, too. No sense using stuff that might break in transit.

June returned from securing her chickens, followed by Atlas.

Erica petted Attie before following Ben's mom back into the kitchen. She spotted a farmhouse-style bench with an old-looking hardwood top on one side of their dining room table. Chairs were at each end and on the other side of the table, making the mismatch rather charming.

She stepped in for a closer look at the bench. Its legs were distressed white pillars that resembled something she'd seen on the porches of Victorian homes on the east side of Marquette. It was a stunning piece.

Erica ran her hand along the top. She'd never coveted anything like she did this bench. It might be a little big, but it'd go so nicely in her tiny home. "This is beautiful. Where did you get it?"

"Ben made it."

"He made it?" Erica didn't know Ben made furniture. "Wow."

June's face looked tight. "He made it for his wife, but she didn't like it, so it's mine now."

That news made her heart pinch. How could she not like it? Especially if he'd made it specifically for her. Poor Ben.

"Lori had very modern taste," June added, as if she'd just spoken badly of her ex-daughter-in-law and needed to backpedal.

"Well, I love it." Erica stared at the bench a little longer.

Did that mean Ben liked older styles? Funny, but she'd never appreciated Bob's mid-1970s home. It was a beautifully built split-level that was functional, but had none of the charm she loved in early twentieth–century homes.

"I don't think I can part with it now," June said.

Erica laughed. "Do I look that greedy for it?"

June laughed, too. "You do. How would you like to make a green salad?"

"I'd love to." Erica stepped up to the big porcelain sink and washed her hands. "Point me in the direction of your large bowls and I'll get to work."

June opened a bottom cupboard. "In here. And, of course, all the fixings are in the fridge."

Erica dug out lettuce and other veggies she'd found in the crisper. June's garden tomatoes were lined up along the windowsill over the sink. Grabbing a paring knife, she got to work rinsing and cutting the salad ingredients. And then Ben and Jason entered the kitchen.

Atlas immediately ran to Ben and sat at his feet.

Ben scratched behind the dog's ears.

Jason reached into the sink to wash his hands, but June swatted him with a towel. "Usc the powder room, please."

"Yes, ma'am." Jason winked at her and headed for the bathroom near the laundry area.

Ben stood in the middle of the big kitchen looking lost. Or maybe sad. He had a strange expression on his face that Erica couldn't decipher.

"What's wrong, dear?" his mom asked.

Ben scratched his chin. "Not a thing. I'm going to feed Attie."

Erica turned back to making a salad, but she heard Ben banging around in the laundry area before she heard the chinking sound of dog kibble being dropped into a bowl. Next came water.

"Nimm futter," Ben said softly.

Erica heard Atlas dig in, his dog tags tinkling against the metal bowl. And then Ben was right next to her, washing his hands in the kitchen sink as if his mom had never told Jason not to.

Ignoring the odd hum of awareness that ripped through her at his sudden nearness, she asked, "What's *neem footer* mean?"

He grabbed a towel hanging over the sink to dry his hands. "Eat food."

"He waits for you to tell him to eat?"

Ben nodded. "Yeah. He's a patient fellow."

"Amazing."

He peeked at her bowl of salad, and snitched a piece of fresh cucumber. "Looks pretty good."

"Thanks." As if she had anything to do with making a cucumber taste good, but she didn't know what else to say.

For some reason, that small gesture seemed far too intimate. It took her back decades, when they'd take bites of food off each other's plates. Did he think of those times? Was that why he'd looked lost earlier, watching her at his mother's kitchen sink? Was he thinking of those times past?

She was simply staying for dinner. That didn't mean she was after anything from him. But part of her longed for more, and that part couldn't articulate exactly what *more* she wanted. Still, something was missing from her life. Missing big-time. What if Ben was a piece of that puzzle?

Chapter Seven

Dinner was long over and Jason had called it a night to escape to his place, leaving just the four of them seated around the picnic table. Ben thought the late July evening air mild, but when Erica had rubbed her arms, his dad didn't hesitate to build a sizable fire in their screened outdoor firepit situated in the corner of the deck.

The heat did feel good. It was after nine and Erica still hadn't gone home. Of course, his parents had invited her to stay and play cribbage, so she did. She had partnered with his mom during the card game and the two of them had trounced him and his dad pretty good.

Erica had always been comfortable with his parents and it appeared that was still the case. His parents had been sorry to see them break up all those years ago. They'd never really faulted Erica, and had encouraged Ben to give her some space. Too bad he hadn't listened.

"We're going to get a nice sunset." His mom pointed at the western horizon, where the sun hung low in the sky. The surrounding clouds were already changing to a peachy pink color.

"Want to switch partners?" his dad asked.

"Sure," Erica agreed. "For a little while. After the sun sets, I should head for home."

Finally. And yet part of him didn't want her to leave. All night he'd felt this tug-of-war inside, hoping she'd go and hoping she'd stay.

"Erica, you partner up with Ben. See if you can help him win a few hands," his mom teased.

"Then let's switch seats." Ben got up to take his dad's place so that he was facing Erica as his partner.

His back was to the sunset, but even the clouds overhead were turning a purple hue. The color reminded him of Erica's thumb, so he glanced at her hands as she shuffled the cards before she passed the deck over to his dad. She wasn't favoring her left hand any longer, so it must be better, even though the skin was still discolored.

Facing Erica wasn't any easier than sitting next to her. He watched the way the late-evening sun caught and shimmered in her dark brown hair. She still wore it pulled back in a ponytail, but tendrils of silky darkness framed her face. He wondered if her hair felt as thick as it used to between his fingers.

He'd sat next to her all evening with Atlas stretched out on the deck between their chairs. He'd accidently run his hand over hers when trying to pet Attie. She'd already been absently stroking the dog's fur. Atlas, the traitor, didn't move with him, but stayed next to Erica. Attie had loved her from the get-go and it wasn't hard to see why.

There was something positive about her. Erica had the sunny disposition of a genuinely grateful person, even though she'd experienced loss, as well. She'd also lost fulfillment in her current job at the hospital. Was it only that, or something else that made her sell her home of over twenty-five years and accept a traveling-nurse position?

Why'd he get the feeling she was running away, maybe from memories of the man she'd married, instead of him?

His dad dealt and after they'd all thrown in a card to his crib, and cut the deck, Ben started the first hand by leading with a nine of clubs. "Nine."

His mom laid down a seven of hearts and called out the tally. "Sixteen."

Ben stared down Erica, hoping she'd play an eight for a run of three points.

"Plus eight equals twenty-four for three." Erica grinned at him.

"You got the message," he said.

"I know how to play."

He raised an eyebrow at her snarky comeback. He didn't want to admit how much he liked their back-and-forth banter. They'd been close friends as kids, before they'd been more, so it shouldn't be a surprise that he liked the woman she'd become without him. There was a new strength in her that drew him.

A sudden disturbance near the barn caused the chickens to screech and squawk. Atlas leaped from the deck before Ben could command him to stay.

"What's that?" Erica stood.

His dad went inside and seconds later came back out with a rifle.

"No, Dad, you might hit Attie." Ben took off after his partner of eight years, dreading what the dog might face. Black bears were known to be in the area, as well as wolves...supposedly. Ben didn't like Attie's chances with either.

"Atlas, halt!" Ben called as he ran toward the chicken coop, but it didn't do any good. Atlas was heading for the tree line.

His father ran behind him, as did Erica. His mom remained on the deck, and he figured that she might be scared. She loved her chickens, but she loved Attie even more.

When they got to the coop, Atlas had returned and was circling the structure and wire fencing, sniffing along the ground.

The sun had set, making the light soft and fading. Ben scanned the area and spotted a very blond tail disappear into the trees. He pointed toward it. "Did you see that?"

His dad chuckled. "Yes, it's a coyote. I thought we might have one poking around, but I never saw him. This has happened before."

Relief filled him. Not a wolf. Or a bear. Ben felt Erica's hand on his shoulder. Had he been that transparent, or did she have too much insight into the bitter-cold fear that had just run through him?

"You okay?" she asked.

"Yeah." He let out his breath with a whoosh. "In all the years I watched Atlas apprehend perps, or go first into buildings to search for drugs or explosives, I knew he'd be okay. He was well-trained, but also street-smart. I had to deal with it because that was our job. But there are wild things up here that he's not used to messing with."

Erica lightly rubbed his back before slipping her hand away. "Now what?"

Ben was half-tempted to ask her to touch him again, maybe even work out the knots between his shoulder blades, but that wasn't a good idea. Not at all. Besides, he had Atlas to tend to. "Attie, what do you think you're doing? *Hier*."

Instead of coming to him, Atlas lay down in front of the gate to the wire fence and raised his head in defiance.

Ben ran a hand through his hair. His partner was officially on duty. This was about guarding the henhouse and who was he to deny the dog the chance to work instead of play? "Okay, Attie. You win."

His mom came near. "I better lock those chickens inside tonight."

"Mom, do you have a pop-up tent?"

"Somewhere, why?"

"I'm camping out here with Attie. We're going to see if that coyote comes back."

His dad handed him the rifle. "You'll want this."

"Okay, but first, let me get that tent." He glanced at Erica. "I guess that ends our game of cribbage."

She smiled, looking far too pretty and even a little wistful. "That's okay. It's past time for me to head home. Stay safe, okay? Both of you."

Ben smiled back. "It's what we do. See you tomorrow."

"Yup."

He watched her for a second or two as she bid goodnight to his folks. The strands of little lights his parents hung along the rails of the deck flicked on from their automatic timer, shedding some light into the backyard. Ben went into action. He had an overnight stakeout to arrange. He glanced at Atlas and the dog seemed to have a sparkle in his eye.

Ben laughed. "Attie, my boy, I feel the same way."

Erica entered her big house with a heavy heart. She'd wanted to stay with Ben and Atlas, and had to bite her tongue to keep from asking him for a second sleeping bag. She wasn't a kid anymore and hanging with Ben overnight wouldn't be a child's sleepover. Wanting to stay, in and of itself, was completely inappropriate. What was wrong with her?

The truth was that staying in a pop-up tent with Ben would have been far more welcoming than entering this house all alone once again. It wasn't that she didn't have friends in the area, and she had the church, too, but she had no family here. She had nothing but memories that crept up on her and stole away her contentment, making her long for better times.

After throwing her purse on the kitchen table, Erica made her way through a trail of boxes and ran upstairs for a shower. Once dried and dressed in pajamas, she climbed into bed and clicked on the TV. Flicking through channels, she stopped on a Christmas-in-July romantic-movie marathon.

It didn't take long to get pulled into the story of an engaged young woman who falls for her new boss. The parallels to her past twisted into her thoughts and Erica revisited choosing Bob Laine over Ben. She'd been young and completely unprepared for the attraction she'd felt for the handsome and very single doctor, who'd praised her nursing skills when she interned at the hospital.

He'd been much older than Erica, so when they'd share coffee breaks, she'd never considered that Bob might have been interested in her. Until he asked her out to dinner…

Erica shook off the memory. She didn't regret her choice. She'd had a good marriage with Bob. Together they'd raised two strong and independent daughters. Maybe too independent, Erica mused. Her girls didn't need her.

Erica still missed her late husband, even though it had been over four years since Bob had been the same man she'd married. But she couldn't help but wonder what life might have been like had she stayed with Ben. Would they have stayed in Pine? Would they have even stayed together?

She wondered if the coyote had returned, and she picked up her phone in order to text Ben. Releasing a sigh, Erica realized the number she had belonged to Jason. She'd have to wait until tomorrow to find out. It was probably a good thing she didn't have Ben's number. Late-night phone calls between them might be hazardous to a good night's sleep. She might find it easier to talk openly with Ben over the phone than in person.

The last thing she needed was giving in to her attraction to Ben Fisher. Renewing their friendship was one thing, but anything more was out of the question. First, he wasn't a believer. And secondly, she was leaving Pine to see the country, like she'd always dreamed of doing.

Propping up her pillows, she leaned back and watched the rest of the movie, shutting out all thoughts of Ben and Atlas and the adventure they might be having as they guarded June Fisher's henhouse. It wasn't long before Erica's eyelids drooped and she fell asleep.

Erica woke with a start. Glancing at the clock, she jumped up out of bed. She was going to be late. She threw back the covers, then spotted the TV remote next to her and clicked it off. She quickly brushed her teeth and hair, and then got dressed.

She didn't have time to make a sandwich, but knew June wouldn't mind making one extra for her. Erica rushed out the door and five minutes later, she was pulling into the Fishers' driveway. She parked on the grass near the workshop and got out.

Bounding into the big open pole barn with country

music blaring from the radio, Erica apologized. "Sorry, I'm late."

No response.

Jason was on the phone in his small office, so she sidled up near where Ben stood looking over tiny-home plans. "How'd it go last night?"

He nodded toward a tray. "There's still coffee."

"Oh, good. I didn't get a chance to make some." Erica poured a cup. "So?"

"Late night?" Ben grumbled.

"No." Was he annoyed that she was late? She was only pushing half an hour. "So did the coyote come back?"

Ben finally looked at her. "He did."

Erica grimaced. "Did you have to shoot him?"

He shook his head. A hint of a smile hovered at the corners of his mouth. "Between you and me, I couldn't."

Erica's heart warmed despite his grumpy demeanor when she'd first arrived. "Big-city cop like you—why not?"

Ben chuckled. "I saw the terror in that mongrel's eyes when he spotted Atlas charging at him. Honestly, I think Attie wanted to play, but he did his duty and chased the coyote away. Dad thinks that with Atlas around, it might be enough to *keep* him away."

"I hope so."

"Yeah, me, too. Even so, they're keeping the hens in the coop for a couple of days. If anything happens to Mom's chickens, I'll never hear the end of it."

She placed her hand on his shoulder, felt the heat there and decided not to linger. "Well, I commend you for showing restraint."

"Like coyotes, do you?"

Erica shrugged. "They're beautiful animals."

"Can be dangerous, carry mange, distemper and rabies."

"But this one didn't," Erica responded. "I mean, you let him go."

"He looked in fine health. A young one, though. Probably having trouble catching game, so he was hoping for something easy like Mom's chickens."

"And then he saw Attie." Erica grinned as the dog made his way toward her. "Good boy, Atlas. Sounds like you had an exciting night."

The dog circled her, and then sat on her foot, his tongue lolling out of his mouth.

"How about you?" Ben looked away, as if he didn't really want to know. "What did you do after you left?"

Erica wouldn't admit to wanting to text him for news, so she shrugged. "I fell asleep watching TV. I didn't even set my alarm."

Ben laughed. "Sounds a lot like my nights."

"Except for last night," Erica corrected.

"Yeah. Except for last night. You should have seen Attie. He was pretty serious about it at first, until he saw a potential playmate." Ben's hazel eyes shone with amusement.

Erica would have loved to have been there. She'd wanted to stay, but there was no way she'd tell him that. A thought suddenly occurred to her. "Do you think he's lonely? Like, for his other K-9s from your department?"

"I don't know. Maybe. Atlas has always been very social. Good with people and dogs alike. He has a great sense of who's a threat and who's not."

"Well, I just love him to pieces." Erica kneeled so she could give Atlas a full on hug.

"He loves you, too." Ben's voice had softened. "And he's a good judge of character."

"Well, thank you, Attie. That means a lot." Erica looked up at Ben. "Has he ever been wrong?"

Ben's gaze intensified. "Nope."

"Good to know." Erica sipped her coffee. Atlas adored Ben, so that spoke for his character as well, but she already knew that. Ben was a good guy, despite the roughness around the edges.

"Okay, coffee break over. Let's get to work." Jason had come in from his small office.

And just in time, too, before Erica asked Ben if he agreed with his dog's opinion of her.

Later that afternoon, Ben was starting to worry about Erica. She was far too quiet. Even at lunch, she'd been less than her usual chatty self. This morning, he and Jason had roughed in the electrical in *The Wanderer*, while Erica finished staining the siding for the twenty-footer.

Jason had hired a guy to set up both the water and gas lines, and then an inspector was scheduled for tomorrow to sign off on all the wiring before they could insulate and ultimately finish the interior of Erica's place.

With Jason tied up with the plumbing guy, Ben joined Erica to help finish staining the siding.

"Everything okay?" He let it slip out before he thought better of it. He really shouldn't dig, or care.

"Yeah, why?"

"You're a little quiet today."

She laughed. "Because I've been staining in here while you and Jason work on mine."

True, but she still wasn't quite herself. "Nothing else, then?"

Erica looked away.

There was something going on. "I know it's none of my business—"

"No, it's not that." She stared at the siding panels, but her hands had stilled. The bruise at the base of her thumb looked better, less purple and more greenish-yellow in hue. It was healing. "I guess I'm feeling the stress of moving. Of leaving behind all that I've ever known and..."

Ben tipped his head, hoping she'd look up at him. "And?"

She resumed applying the stain in long, even brushstrokes. "It's been really nice working here, with your son and your parents—they are so warm and welcoming. I forgot what it's like to be around a family."

Ben felt the sorrow in her voice and it cut through him, along with the fact that she hadn't included him in her list of reasons for liking to work here. "Where do your daughters live?"

"Ashley's in Colorado and Emily's in Florida."

"So, far away."

"Yes." Her eyes clouded over.

"Can I ask you something personal?"

"Sure."

"Are you and your daughters close?"

Erica shrugged. "Not like we used to be, but they're grown now, with their own lives. We talk on the phone regularly, but that's not the same as in person, you know?"

"Yeah." Ben knew.

He'd missed his son when Jason had gone off to college in Marquette, never to move back home. He missed his daughter now, having only short phone calls with her since the divorce had been finalized. He thought about how much his parents had missed him and his heart pinched. He'd been too busy with his career and hiding his pain to visit regularly. Now that he'd been home these past couple of months, it felt as if this was where he was meant to be. Funny, because he even missed Lori. Not so much wished they were still married, but hoped she was okay. He wanted her happy even though he'd been unable to make her so.

He wanted Erica happy, too, and right now she looked anything but. "Hey, what are you doing this Saturday?"

She gave him an odd look, like he should know. "I work on Saturdays, remember? Mondays and Tuesdays, too."

"Yes, but what time do you get off work?"

She narrowed her dark eyes. "Why?"

"Would you like to meet me at the Pine Fair afterward?"

Erica looked taken aback by the request.

He was surprised he'd asked her. "Look, it's not a date or anything. Jason and I are going, and I thought maybe you'd like to join us. You know, a team-building thing."

Erica burst out laughing. "Team-building. Really?"

He laughed, too. "Okay, that was weak. But the offer still stands. You look like you could use some fun." He knew he could, too.

"Okay. Sure. My shift ends at seven, so I could meet you there by eight, say in front of the Ferris wheel?"

"Sounds good. Why don't you give me your cell number in case something comes up?" Ben pulled his phone out of his back pocket.

Erica rattled off her number. "Call mine, so I have yours. My phone's in my car."

Ben punched New Contact, plugged in the number and hit Save. Then he called her until her voice mail message clicked on. "Don't forget to meet me at the Pine Fair Ferris wheel Saturday night at eight."

"Nice." Erica's cheeks were pink.

"It's a date. Not a date." He felt like an idiot, but hung it out there, anyway. "Unless you want it to be."

Fortunately, Erica didn't laugh. She just shook her head and kept staining.

Even though Jason would be around, unless he met up with some friends, it sure felt like a date. And Ben had been transported back to his teens, when he'd stammered out a request for Erica to go to the homecoming dance with him. She'd been the prettiest girl there, wearing a red dress that had made her skin look warm and golden.

Even if it ended up as a date, was that so bad? He could use an evening out with a beautiful woman by his side. The fact that Erica was leaving reminded him to keep things friendly. He could do that.

For both their sakes, he had to do that.

Chapter Eight

After her last rounds on the floor, Erica ducked into the ladies' locker room at the end of her shift on Saturday. That morning, she'd fussed over what to wear and had finally packed a pair of light denim capris and a boat-necked shirt that was lemon-yellow with white stripes and a pair of comfy yellow flip-flops.

Once changed, she brushed her teeth, then her hair. Tipping her head this way and that in the mirror, Erica decided to leave her hair down. It fell a little past her shoulders with a natural wave that hid the indentation of the clip she'd worn all day. A quick swipe of peach-tinted lip gloss and she was ready to head for the Pine Fair and meet Ben.

And Jason, too, but Erica had a feeling he wouldn't hang around them much.

She blew out her breath. Was this even a good idea?

"Wow, don't you look nice." One of her nurses had just ended her shift, as well. "Got a date?"

Remembering Ben's statement that it wasn't a date unless she wanted it to be, she answered, "Thanks, I think it might be."

Her coworker wiggled her eyebrows. "Well, have fun."

"I will." That was what had her worried. Just how much fun would she have with Ben?

"Oh, and thanks again for catching that medication mix-up. Still don't know how it got switched."

"That's what I'm here for." Erica nodded. She knew the patients on her floor, and she often verified any med-order changes before they went out. Good thing, too. "Have a great night, Sheila."

"You, too, Erica."

Erica grabbed her duffel bag and slung her purse over her shoulder. She walked into the hallway, then to a door leading to the parking lot. Exiting the overly air-conditioned hospital, she breathed in the fresh, summer-night air. It was a warm evening with a soft breeze, perfect for the last Saturday night in July.

A tingle of anticipation zipped up her spine. Erica needed a night of simple fun and she looked forward to experiencing that with Ben. Maybe a little more than she should, but then they'd attended the Pine Fair together many times in the past—as friends and as a couple. Tonight was bound to be different. They were neither friends, like they used to be, nor a couple.

After starting her car, she suppressed any and all qualms by cranking up the radio. It wasn't long before she was singing along to an old song by Bon Jovi, feeling lighter than she had in a long time. It was just a small-town fair and Erica had gone to it many times, but it had been years since she'd been there with Ben.

The half-hour drive went quickly, and soon Erica was looking for a parking spot near the farmer's market lot, where Pine's three-day carnival, always held over the last weekend in July, had been set up. Lights flashed in the waning sunlight and the rickety noise of a tiny roller coaster filled the air.

Erica found a parking spot and pulled in. She turned off the engine, then took a deep breath, grabbed her small purse and pulled it over her head so it hung across her body. She locked the car and headed for the Ferris wheel.

The Ferris wheel was a large one for a rinky-dink town fair. It was also easy to see from where she parked. Red, green and yellow lights danced and shimmied to some preset pulse. The smell of fried food hit her next and her stomach rumbled. She'd skipped her dinner break.

Tempted to grab a quick corn dog, she checked her watch. It was nearly eight o'clock. She didn't want to be late, so she kept walking. She spotted Ben before he saw her, giving her a chance to study him. He stood tall but at ease, watching people as they passed by. He wore a simple T-shirt with jeans, but he looked every bit the police officer he used to be. Strong and alert, as if ready to jump into action if needed. She shuddered to think what kind of *action* he'd seen. Attie, too. Jason wasn't with him and Erica found herself glad of that.

When he noticed her, she smiled. "Hello."

He smiled back, making the skin at the corners of his eyes crinkle. "Hi."

"No Jason?"

"He went with some friends. I hope you don't mind."

Erica shook her head. "Not at all. So what do you want to do first? Rides, games, food?"

Ben chuckled. A warm, relaxed sound. "I thought we could walk around a bit. Are you hungry?"

"Actually, I am."

"Me, too. What would you like? I seem to remember you were fond of corn dogs."

Erica laughed. "Still am. Although, I'd rather have something a little more substantial. I sort of skipped my dinner break."

Ben's eyes looked concerned. "Emergency?"

"Yes and no. I had to sort out some medication confusion, and then a woman who'd had minor surgery suffered a seizure from a weird electrolyte imbalance. She stabilized."

"Wow. Sounds like a busy day." Ben smiled.

"It was, so now I'm starved."

"Come on, I know the perfect place. I saw it when I came in." He reached for her hand.

Erica took it, surprised that they were holding hands as if it was the most natural thing in the world. But it wasn't. This was odd and sweet, and Erica's stomach flipped when she felt Ben's thumb trail across the back of her hand.

Oh, boy.

They stopped near a food truck that offered smoked barbecue choices with all the sides a person might wish for. The aroma coming out of that truck made her mouth water.

"How's this?" Ben asked.

"Looks good to me." Erica scanned the chalkboard menu and picked the smoked brisket with a side of mac and cheese.

Ben ordered the sampler platter, then dug in to his back pocket for his wallet.

Erica opened her purse.

"I've got this." Ben waved her away.

"Then this really is a date." Erica grinned.

Ben laughed. "Yes, ma'am, I suppose it is."

That merry look in his eyes made her feel like a teenager again. Back then, their dates had always ended with kisses. Would this one, too? Her pulse skipped a beat. Should she allow it? They were older now and knew better than to get involved when she was leaving, but it had been so long since she'd been held, let alone kissed. Nope, better not. This night was supposed to be fun and kissing would only complicate things between them.

It didn't take long to get their food. With steaming plates and soft drinks in hand, they made their way to a picnic table. Erica was ready to dig in when she noticed that Ben was waiting. "What?"

"Aren't you going to say grace?"

She hadn't planned on it. "I will, if you'd like."

He shrugged. "Sure."

Erica closed her eyes. "Thank You, Lord, for this food and let us have a good night. Amen."

"Amen," he said with a smile.

She should have asked for wisdom, too, because she kept thinking about kissing Ben. Concentrating on the meal before her, Erica took a big bite of brisket and her eyes nearly rolled back in her head as she chewed. Finally, she said, "This is so good."

"Yeah? Is it hot enough?" His eyes held a hint of mischief.

"Yes. The food temperature is good." Funny that he'd remember that. Wiping her mouth with a napkin, she asked, "So what's with you wanting me to pray over our food?"

He shrugged. "Living with my parents, I've gotten used to it. It's sort of nice."

"Do you go with them to their church?"

"No."

Erica went out on a limb. "Want to go with me to mine tomorrow morning?"

"You don't stop, do you?" Ben's hazel eyes teased, but he didn't look the least bit annoyed like the last time she'd asked.

Erica raised her hands in surrender. "Hey, you brought up saying grace. I just thought maybe..."

"Maybe I will go with you. Maybe church is what I need."

Was he referencing his divorce as the reason for attending? Whatever the reason, Ben had thrown down a challenge of sorts, so she picked it up. "Jesus is who you need." Erica pointed with her plastic knife for emphasis. "He's all any of us need."

Ben narrowed his gaze. "When did you get so religious?"

"Religion is man-made. Faith is different. It's a gift we choose to accept. But, to answer your question, I found myself leaning on God when Bob got sick. I was hoping that God would heal him like He'd done for my patient with the tumor."

"Sick?" Ben looked like he'd not heard about what had happened to her husband that ultimately ended his life.

"He had a massive stroke. I had to quit my job to become his full-time caregiver."

Ben reached out his hand to cover hers. "Erica, I'm so sorry. I didn't know that."

She gave his hand a squeeze before letting go. It was no surprise that he hadn't known, living so far away. Only those closest to her knew how serious it had been. She hadn't wanted to advertise her plight and the hospital had been very gracious in giving her a leave of absence for however long she needed.

"It was the hardest time of my life. I still wonder why God allowed it all to happen, or why that healing never came."

"And yet you still believe."

Erica nodded. "God is God. He knows a much bigger timeline than I do. I choose to trust Him even when things don't go my way."

"Hmm." Ben seemed to be considering that statement.

"We live in an imperfect world, a fallen one, so I can't expect difficulties to never touch me."

"Bad things can happen to good people," he said with a defeated tone in his voice.

"But good things do, too." Erica considered tonight a good thing because Ben seemed more like the man she'd known so long ago. She didn't want to spoil the evening with her sad story so she changed the subject. "What's Atlas doing tonight?"

"Hanging with Millie and my folks."

"No guarding the henhouse?"

Ben looked thoughtful. "Nope. He was lying near Millie when I left."

"He's such a sweet dog. I can't imagine him apprehending anyone."

Ben beamed with pride. "Atlas didn't mess around. He was fast as lightning. He was an excellent K-9 but I worry that he might miss having a job to do. I'd like to find something more for him. The right place, but I'm not sure what that might be."

"You'll figure it out in time. What about you? Do you miss being a cop?" Erica didn't want to seem nosy, but she wanted to know.

Ben shrugged, looking away. "Sometimes."

He didn't elaborate, or appear comfortable with where

the conversation was going, so Erica moved on to her mac and cheese.

"I will admit to being more relaxed since I retired."

Erica wouldn't consider Ben laid-back, so if this was relaxed, she'd rather not see him stressed out.

When they'd finished their food, Ben gathered up their plates and tossed them in the trash. Then he reached for her hand again. "Come on, I think we need to ride that Ferris wheel."

Erica complied, slipping her hand in his. She wasn't about to turn down the chance to see her hometown at sunset from the top of the Ferris wheel. And considering the warmth she felt from just holding Ben's hand, being snuggled next to him in the small two-seater pod wouldn't be bad, either. In fact, she was looking forward to it.

Ben thought about what Erica had said about Atlas missing his fellow K-9s. Should he look into a trainer and see if Attie could be of training help? But then Ben would need to be there, too, and daytime wouldn't work for Jason. Ben didn't want to leave his son hanging, or miss out on the work. He rather enjoyed it. Still, he needed to do more for his retired partner than simply play fetch.

By the time they reached the Ferris wheel, Ben still hadn't let go of Erica's hand. He wasn't sure what had prompted him to reach for her, but once he'd made that connection, he didn't want to let go. He was surprised and more than a little pleased that Erica hadn't let go, either.

Being around Erica these last couple of weeks had brought him out of the daze he'd been in for a good portion of the year. Lori leaving him had been a kick in the gut he hadn't expected. These past seven months, Ben had wallowed about how he'd failed at marriage. It hurt, sure, but he was beginning to think his pride had been wounded worse than his heart. He'd locked up that part of him tight a long time ago.

Erica had experienced her share of grief and sorrow, yet she'd kept a sunny demeanor. She hadn't folded in on herself; instead, she'd found a strong faith in God. He'd go to Erica's church and check it out. Maybe there was something there for him. Something that might heal the old wounds and the new one his divorce had opened.

They were up next in the Ferris-wheel line, so Ben waited while the ride attendant lifted the bar to their little passenger pod. He let Erica climb in first, then sat next to her. There wasn't much leg room, so he had to turn a little in the seat to fit. He didn't mind; it gave him a better view of Erica's face. She didn't seem to mind his knees nearly knocking into hers. The attendant replaced the bar, and the pod swung back and forth as the ride moved forward.

"This is fun," Erica said with a smile.

She looked beautiful with her hair down. The soft breeze tousled her brown locks, making him itch to run his fingers through those loose waves. He rested his arm along the back of their seat instead.

The ride stopped, leaving them swinging gently as the next pod was loaded. It made him chuckle. "I haven't been on one of these in ages."

"Remember when we used to come here as kids?" Erica asked.

"Of course, I do. You loved the swings and the Ferris wheel, but never the Tilt-A-Whirl."

"Because you cranked the wheel way too hard. It made me sick to my stomach."

Ben laughed. “That was the whole point.”

“To get me sick? Nice.” But she laughed at the memory, too, and then looked thoughtful. “Thanks for inviting me.”

“Thanks for coming.” Ben turned a little more, so he could face her. “Can I ask you a question?”

“Sure.”

Gathering up his courage, he asked something that had plagued him for many years. “What did I do that made you break off our engagement?”

Erica looked down at her hands and twisted her wedding ring. “It wasn’t you, Ben. I was so young and completely unprepared for the attraction I felt for Bob. It scared me. It made me doubt our relationship.”

“And I didn’t listen very well when you told me, did I?” Ben had gotten angry and they’d argued.

She’d merely asked for some space to figure things out, but he’d flown off the handle, accusing her of being unfaithful. Deep down, he knew she hadn’t been. Why else would she have come to him with questions and confusion? He’d taken it all completely wrong, thinking she’d wanted to end it. End them.

“No.” Her voice was whisper-quiet. “After you left the area without a word, I figured we weren’t meant to be.”

“I’ve always been sorry about that.” He gave in and tucked a strand of her hair behind her ear. “I should have stayed and fought for you.”

Her dark gaze reached right into his soul, convicting him of not caring enough to keep her. “Why didn’t you?”

The million-dollar question. “I was young, too. Immature and hotheaded.”

Erica nodded. Despite his part in their breakup, she

didn't hold it against him. She probably never had. "But then you found someone you loved, yes?"

"Lori?" Ben snorted. "We had to get married. She was pregnant with Jason and I wanted my son raised in a two-parent household. I grew to love her. I think she loved me as well, but obviously we couldn't keep it going. She left me for a guy she worked with."

Erica winced. "I'm sorry."

Ben shrugged. He'd accepted his part in not keeping it going. "She deserved better, and maybe now, she'll have it."

"But, you do, too. I'm sorry for the way I handled things back then."

He nodded. "Yeah, me, too."

"Did you ever wonder what our lives might have been like had we stayed together?" Erica looked out over the view of their hometown against the soft colors of a summer sunset. They were stopped at the top and the light breeze was still messing with her hair.

"I tried not to." Ben tucked the strands behind her ear again, anything to touch her without crossing the line of friendship. "I guess we'll never know."

Erica wore a wistful expression when she faced him. "No. I guess not."

The ride jerked suddenly, and Erica gripped his knee. "Yikes, that didn't feel right."

The wheel smoothed out, but she hadn't removed her hand. The heat of her palm radiated through the fabric of his jeans and he had to admit that her hand felt more than right where it was. Encouraged, he tipped up her chin with his fingertips and slowly leaned toward her, ready to pull back if she didn't welcome him. But she didn't move.

Her eyes grew wide before dropping downward in anticipation, so Ben stayed on course. He let his lips lightly touch hers, as if she was made of spun sugar. As if she might dissolve into thin air like the cotton candy they'd passed if he pressed too hard.

Erica's lips were soft and she surprised him by threading her fingers into his hair until they were resting at the back of his head. Pulling him closer, she kissed him fully and there was nothing light or fluffy about it.

Whoa!

This was exactly what they shouldn't be doing. Kissing Erica deeply crossed the line into dangerous territory. She was leaving. He was staying.

Irritation for his weakness seared through him, so he broke the kiss and sat back. "Erica, I'm sorry."

For a split second, she looked hurt...and then relieved. She held up her hand. "Don't be. Not when I kicked it up a notch."

He chuckled. "And a very nice notch it was, but we both know this isn't going to work."

Even if she wasn't leaving, he was still coming to terms with his divorce. The fact that Lori had left him for someone else really did hurt, and kissing Erica felt too much like he was lashing out at Lori. Maybe even punishing Erica for leaving him, too...

"I get it. I'm leaving."

"Not just that, but a long-distance thing wouldn't really work."

"No, I suppose not," she replied.

"Friends still?"

"Of course. We'll always be friends." Her gaze was earnest and genuine.

"Good." He valued her as a friend. Talking to her helped, but could he really tell her everything? Maybe—

The ride spun quickly, once, then twice around. It was the telltale sign it was almost over and the attendant had given them all this last little thrill.

Erica's hair flew up, then forward. She laughed.

So did he.

They enjoyed the end of the ride and then walked around a bit more. When Jason joined them to say he was heading home, Ben knew it wise to return with his son. Having Erica drop him off at his parents' place wasn't a good idea. He didn't trust himself not to repeat that kiss they'd shared at the top of the Ferris wheel, because deep down, Ben didn't want to be *just friends* with Erica. He wanted much, much more.

"So how was your evening with Erica?" Jason asked with a goofy grin as he started up his truck.

Ben chuckled. "It was fine."

"You two looked pretty cozy walking around hand in hand."

Ben shrugged. "We're friends."

"Uh-huh." Jason wasn't buying it.

Ben couldn't really sell it, but that was what he was going with for now. They pulled into his parents' driveway and Jason stopped to let him out. Ben held the door as he leaned back in. "Thanks for tonight. For driving and everything."

"Sure thing." Jason leaned forward. "Dad?"

"Yeah?"

His son's gaze was direct and serious. "I'm really glad you're here, working with me."

"I am, too." Ben shut the door and tapped on the truck

hood. Watching his son pull up to his own tiny home, Ben knew that he'd meant what he'd told him. What had initially been coming home to gather his wits after the divorce was turning into something that had the makings of permanence. Ben believed that he wanted to stay for good.

He walked into a quiet house and noted that his mom had left the light on over the sink. Following the ray of light down the entrance hall, he stepped into the kitchen and spotted Atlas lying near Millie. His parents' dog must not have wanted to make the climb upstairs. Had he been home earlier, Ben would have carried her up. But she looked peaceful on her memory foam bed and Ben didn't want to wake his parents moving her around.

He kneeled down and scratched Millie behind her ears. "You're a good old girl."

Millie opened her eyes for a moment, then closed them.

Atlas nudged under Ben's hand for pets, too.

He obliged, then stood back up to get a glass of lemonade. Once poured, Ben sat down at the kitchen table, keeping his gaze on the two dogs. Atlas stayed close to Millie.

"Attie, what can I do for you? How can I make your transition better?"

Atlas looked at him with wise eyes. If only he could talk.

Ben knew his partner had more to give, more to offer. But in what capacity? Ben was actually glad they were both retired. After nearly two months away from the department, he had to admit he felt more at ease. More relaxed. He certainly felt relief knowing Atlas could settle into being just a dog, but was that what his partner wanted?

Ben downed the last of his lemonade and put the glass in the sink. "Come on, Attie, time for bed."

Atlas groaned and rolled onto his side so that he was touching Millie.

"No?" Ben chuckled. "You're going to stay down here with Millie. You're a good friend, Attie. The best."

Ben went into the family room and grabbed a throw blanket. He returned to Millie's bed. "Up, Attie, *steh*."

The dog stood, and Ben arranged the blanket on the floor next to Millie's bed. He gave Attie a pet. "If you're staying down here, you might as well be comfortable."

Atlas fluffed the blanket with his paws, turned once, twice, then lay down.

Ben used the downstairs bathroom before heading for his room. Passing by his parents' bedroom, he noticed their door was open just a crack and he could hear their window fan on low. Everything else was quiet. Peaceful. He entered his room, shut the door and changed into pajama bottoms before climbing into bed.

Lying there, he knew sleep would elude him for a while yet. What waited for him at Erica's church service? Would he find something he needed? He hoped so. With his arms crossed behind his head, Ben stared at the ceiling and threw down a challenge. "God, if You're out there, show me something, anything, so I'll know You're real."

Chapter Nine

The next morning as Erica was about to walk out the door to go pick up Ben for church, she got a text from him.

Erica, I'm going to be late. I'll meet you at your church if you give me the address.

Reading it a second time, she got an empty feeling in the pit of her stomach. He was going to bail on her. Still, she texted back the name and address of the church, but she wouldn't hold her breath. He probably wouldn't show.

Maybe Ben regretted the kiss they'd shared like she did and didn't want to face her. That brief exchange had taken her back to when they were young. It had also made her want more of what they'd once had. More would make leaving Pine that much harder. She couldn't say that she'd fallen back in love with Ben, since part of her had never really stopped loving him.

Erica left her house, hoping it wouldn't get weird while they worked together. She slipped into her car, then worried the whole way to church about how they'd act around each other since they'd shared a kiss.

Once inside the old, charming church building, Erica headed straight for the library table in the small foyer. It held several carafes of both hot coffee and water, along with all the fixings for tea and hot chocolate.

"Hey." Ruth tapped her shoulder.

"Hi." Erica gave her friend a hug and then looked beyond her. "Where are your boys?"

"Bo took them outside until service starts. They're pretty wound up." Ruth rubbed her hands together. "How are you? It's getting close now, huh?"

"Maybe three weeks, or even less, once the tiny home is done." Erica had been counting the days with excitement.

If the truth had been told, the closer that leaving day loomed, the more anxious she felt. She'd really be on her own out there, with no church, and no Ruth or Maddie to lean on for help if she needed it.

"Morning." Ben's deep voice sounded behind her.

Erica turned around fast. "You came."

"I said I would." Ben nodded toward Ruth. "Just late."

"Not late at all. Hi, I'm Ruth." She reached out her hand.

Ben shook it. "Ben Fisher."

Erica tried to calm the butterflies that tumbled inside of her and failed. She couldn't think of a single thing to say.

"Nice to meet you. Well, I better get seated." Ruth gave her a very pointed look as she squeezed her elbow. Hard.

Erica rubbed her arm as she watched her friend walk away for a second or two.

"Friend of yours?" Ben asked with a hint of a smile.

"Yes."

"Sorry about the text, but it was rough at the house this morning."

Erica realized that he didn't look quite right. Alarmed, she asked, "Is everything okay?"

Ben shook his head and his eyes looked a little glassy and red, too. "Millie passed away sometime during the night."

"Oh, no." Erica covered her mouth with her hand, but images of the sweet old golden retriever kept flashing across her mind's eye, making her heart heavy.

Ben ran a hand through his hair. "Yeah. After I got home last night, I couldn't get Attie to come upstairs. He stayed next to Millie, so she wasn't alone. He must have sensed it was coming."

Erica felt the sting of tears just picturing it. The music started, but she didn't want to go into the sanctuary just yet. Between last night's kiss, Ben's obvious attempt to appear unmoved by Millie's death and the stress of leaving, Erica was on the verge of breaking down right there in the foyer.

Ben reached out to her and pulled her into his arms. "I'm sorry for telling you."

She held on tight. With her throat thick and her forehead against his shoulder, she managed to get out a response. "I'm glad you did."

He'd had good reason to text her this morning and here she'd been irritated that he wouldn't show.

Erica breathed in deep to get a handle on the emotions running through her, but instead of letting go, she clung a little tighter. Ben smelled good, too, like fresh air and cedar trees mixed with warm vanilla. She finally pushed away from him, missing how right his arms had felt around her.

He tipped his head toward her. "You okay?"

"Yes. Let's go in and find a seat in the back."

"You lead."

Erica nodded and stepped inside the sanctuary, thinking Ben was exactly right. She needed to take the lead and keep things normal between them. Friendly.

Fortunately, the congregation stood during the song service so it was easy to slip in and find a seat without too much distraction. Although Maddie, as part of the worship team up front on the altar, spotted them and smiled.

After sliding into one of the back pews, Erica felt Ben close beside her. Really? Couldn't he move over? She was already at the edge of the row on her side. But then she noticed Ruth and her two boys, her mother-in-law and husband were piling in behind Ben.

Erica leaned over and whispered, "I thought you were already in here."

Ruth shrugged. "I had to find Bo and the boys."

Bo gave her a smile and a wave.

Erica glanced at Ben, but he didn't seem to mind. When they sat down for the announcements, it was still tight. So tight that Ben had to drape his arm around the back of the pew, grazing her shoulder and making her aware of his every move.

As the pastor delivered a message about spiritual wounds that couldn't be healed through sheer grit, Erica saw Ben lean forward. He was listening with every fiber of his being. She could feel the tension in him when she shifted in her seat and her arm brushed against his. She didn't dare distract him by trying to give him more room. She was still sitting with her leg plastered against his, but Ben didn't seem to notice. He was locked on to every word of the sermon.

Erica closed her eyes and prayed silently for him. Not knowing what to ask for, she simply repeated the phrase *please, Lord*, and then refocused on the message.

When her pastor finally closed with an invitation to visit the altar for prayer, Erica gripped the edge of the pew when Ben stood. He made his way by her to go down front as if nothing could stop him. A few others in the congregation were heading there, too, so at least he wouldn't be down there by himself.

She caught Ruth's gaze, and her friend gave her an encouraging smile.

But Erica didn't feel encouraged. She was uneasy. If Ben became a man of faith, that would only bring them closer. And it would be even harder to remain *just friends*.

Ben had learned long ago not to feel too deeply. *Feelings* had not only let him down, but they also often got in the way of doing what needed to be done, especially at work, so he'd detached from his feelings. Emotional attachments hurt too much when they were severed or lost, so he'd learned to take those hurts and stick them in a figurative box so he wouldn't have to deal with them. In hindsight, he knew that hadn't been wise, but he wasn't sure how to fix it, or how to fix himself.

His decision to give his life to God had been thought-filled, based on the sermon he'd heard, but there'd also been an overwhelming draw to do so. Was that emotion tugging on his heart, or was it God himself? Ben had asked God to reveal Himself, and He had. Ben had never before felt such an overwhelming presence. God had shown up.

And Ben was glad he'd gone forward. Emotionally, he felt lighter, but his thoughts were racing. What did all this mean for him now? Could he really give God his damaged soul and come out better for it in the end? Could he open up his feelings and risk the hurt that brought without being destroyed? Maybe God would show him how.

He opened his eyes and the preacher who'd prayed with him, a younger man than himself, extended his hand. "I'm Pastor Bill Parsons. Welcome."

Ben accepted it for a firm shake. "Ben Fisher."

"New to the area?"

"I grew up here, but have just recently moved back. I was invited to your service by Erica Laine."

"Erica's a special woman," Pastor Bill Parsons said. "She has a lot of wisdom."

"True." In fact, Ben wanted to get back to Erica before she left. Surely, she wouldn't leave without talking to him about all this, and giving him a few pointers. "Well, I've got to run. Nice to meet you, Pastor Bill Parsons."

"It's just Bill." The man smiled and handed him a business card with a penetrating gaze. "If you have any questions about what you did today, call me."

Ben nodded. He wasn't sure what titles preachers went by. He grew up going to a more traditional church, which his parents still attended. One thing he knew for sure—Bill Parsons had genuine eyes. He might take the man up on his offer. "Thanks, Bill."

Ben made his way to the back of the sanctuary. People were milling around, but he spotted Erica and walked toward her. She was talking with two women—Ruth, the redhead from their row, and a blond girl who had been part of the group of singers.

When he reached them, he smiled. "Hello."

"Ben, this is Maddie, also a friend of mine. And you've already met Ruth."

"Yes. Nice to meet you both." He nodded, then turned to Erica. "Ready to go?"

She looked a little surprised. "Um, sure."

He didn't want to talk to Erica's friends, no matter how kind they might be. He was antsy to talk to her. Alone.

The three women shared a look as Erica said her good-byes. She turned to him. "What's your hurry?" Then her eyes softened. "Sorry, did you need to get back home to your folks?"

"No. I was hoping we could grab lunch. I'd like to talk to you about what I just did."

She smiled. "Of course."

"You might as well ride with me, and I can drop you back here afterward."

"Fine." Erica looked a little guarded.

"Anything wrong?"

"No."

He wasn't sure he believed that, but let it go. They walked out into overcast but dry-for-now skies and headed for his SUV. He opened the passenger side for her and she climbed in without a word.

After he slid behind the wheel and started the engine, he turned to her. "Is the Pine diner okay with you?"

"That's perfect."

"Great." He pulled out, then drove a block or so and parked.

Man, she was awfully quiet the whole way. Not that it took long, but still, shouldn't she be cheering him on for going forward? Isn't that what a Bible-thumper was supposed to do? He gripped the steering wheel a moment before shutting off the engine. He got out, ready to open her door, but she was already walking toward the entrance.

He ran his hand through his hair. *She's the one who'd nagged me to come to her church. Is she sorry I came?*

Opening the glass door to the diner, Ben inhaled the smell of fried potatoes and freshly brewed coffee. Once they were seated in a vinyl booth, he knew exactly what he wanted. When the waitress arrived with two glasses of water and menus, he asked, "Are you still serving the rise-'n'-shine breakfast platter?"

"All day, every day." The waitress pulled out her order pad.

"I'd like that with eggs over medium, double sausage patties and pancakes instead of toast."

The waitress looked at Erica.

Erica grinned, finally looking like herself. "I'll take the same but as it comes."

"Coffee?"

"Yes, please," they said in unison and laughed.

"So you still like big breakfasts for lunch." Erica trailed the rim of her water glass with her finger.

"Love them any time of day." He was hungry, too, since he hadn't eaten anything at home. Ben pulled out his phone. "I better text my mom and let her know where I am."

"Send my sympathies."

Ben nodded and did so.

"So Attie stayed with Millie all night?" Erica asked.

"Yeah. He was still lying by her side when my mom found her this morning."

Erica briefly closed her eyes. "If you're looking for a new job for Attie, he'd make a good therapy dog. Giving comfort, and letting folks pet him, you know, like the ones that visit the sick in hospitals? My hospital has a volunteer program for that."

Ben tipped his head. "Really? Maybe I'll check into that."

"I don't think you'll be sorry."

That might be true, although hanging out with sick kids might be tough considering he and Atlas had only visited healthy kids in area schools. He'd at least look into it. The key was how Atlas responded. "So this Pastor Bill Parsons, is he a good guy?"

"Very. He's married with a couple of kids and he facilitates a grief support group on Monday nights. That's where I met Ruth and Maddie."

Of course, she'd gone through a grieving process and support groups were supposed to be helpful. He'd been there, done that, but it hadn't worked for him. The city shrink hadn't helped him when Jack had been killed in an exchange of gunfire. And after what happened with Judge, Ben couldn't be honest with the shrink and expect to keep his job.

"Do you still go?" he asked.

"No. Not anymore."

"Erica." He reached for her hands, glad when she took his and squeezed. "I'm the same man, but different. I'm not one to trust my feelings, or give in to them, but I answered a tug to my heart, so what's next?"

"Start reading the Bible. And tell your family about your newfound faith."

He laughed, because he actually couldn't wait to tell his folks and Jason. Molly, even Lori. What'd he say to his ex-wife, he had no idea, but he knew he needed to make that call. "I guess that makes me a Bible-thumper, too."

Erica laughed. "I guess so. How's it feel?"

Ben shrugged. "Feelings are fickle."

"They can be." Erica didn't let go of his hands. "So don't you trust your feelings?"

He gave a short bark of laughter. "It's not the trusting, it's just plain old feeling and all the hurt that goes with it that I have a problem with."

Erica looked concerned. "What happened to you, Ben?"

"Two partners killed right in front me is what happened." There, he'd said it.

Her pretty brown eyes widened and she looked like she was searching for the right words. "Don't they have people to talk to—"

He cut her off. "Sure they do. I had to see the department counselor, but it's hard to be honest when it's going into your personnel file."

Erica let go of his hands and sat back when the waitress arrived with their food, so he leaned back, too.

Then Erica looked at him. "Would you say grace?"

She wasn't being cheeky or even challenging, so he bowed his head. His first out-loud prayer. "Okay, here goes. God, thank You for drawing me to You. Help me know how to live and bless this breakfast. Amen."

When he looked at Erica, she had tears in her eyes. "What?"

She gave him a watery smile. "Nothing. I'm just happy you've found your way home."

He was, too. Spiritually as well as physically. More and more, he knew remaining in Pine for good was right for him. He enjoyed working with his son and he liked being around for his parents. He owed them big-time. Erica was a big part of finding his way to God, but then what would happen when she left? He'd already gotten too close to her against his better judgment, but she'd wiggled her way in just like when they were kids.

They weren't kids anymore and he wasn't the same guy who'd loved her all those years ago. He didn't know if he could ever love her completely. There'd always be part of him that he held back. The part that had been crushed too many times.

Erica had meant what she'd said. She was very happy for Ben finding faith, so why did she feel like crying? The man was practically beaming, which amazed her, considering what he'd shared about seeing two of his partners killed. Judge must have been one of the two.

Erica's heart twisted. Considering how gentle Ben was with animals, witnessing his first K-9's death must have torn him in two. And he'd bottled up all that pain, pretending it didn't exist. How was that working for him? Not well, she'd guess, but she couldn't push him. Working through his past was something he had to want. It was something that God could stir in him, though. With prayer.

Which brought her back to why she needed to keep her distance. Ben needed time to settle into this new faith-filled life without any romantic distractions from her. But having their faith in common would only make their connection stronger. And that made her nervous. She didn't want to ruin anything between them, or add any more pain into his life. Even so, Erica's feelings for Ben were growing and if she wasn't careful, leaving was going to be pain-filled for her, too.

Maybe more than she could take.

Once they'd finished eating and split the bill—Erica demanded that she'd pay her own way this time—they headed out toward Ben's vehicle.

"How's packing up your house going?" he asked as he opened her door.

"Pretty good." She climbed in.

"Anything you need help with?"

Erica considered his offer. She could use a hand hauling the bigger stuff to her storage unit. "Maybe."

He smiled as he shut her door and then slid in behind the wheel. "Let me know and I'll be there."

"Thank you."

Big, fat raindrops started to fall from the sky, hitting the windshield with a splat. Sporadically at first, and then more insistent until a downpour rattled against the roof. Ben drove slow, his wipers barely keeping up with clearing rain from the glass.

When he pulled next to her car at the church, he shifted into Park and turned toward her. "We can wait it out."

With the rain pouring outside, the inside of Ben's Honda CR-V seemed to shrink in on her. "It's okay, I won't melt."

He gave her a crooked smile and his gaze had darkened. His eyes looked mossy green against the sage-colored shirt he had on. So very handsome, and if she didn't get out of there now—

"You might," he teased.

Be still, my heart!

The way he looked at her made Erica's pulse race. Boy, was she glad for her twelve-hour shifts over the next two days. She needed a little distance from Ben. No, she needed a lot of distance. "I'll see you Wednesday."

Erica dug her keys out of her purse and quickly popped out of Ben's car before she attempted a repeat of last night's kiss. Warm rain pelted her, but she didn't care.

It actually felt good. It washed away the temptation to climb back into Ben's SUV and throw herself at him.

After waving, she slipped into her car, started it and then waited for him to pull onto the road. She followed until they were a couple of miles out of Pine, and then she turned onto her road.

Once home, Erica shut the door. Her house was too quiet, and loneliness enveloped her like a heavy blanket she needed to toss off before she was smothered. Peering out the window at the now steady shower that looked like it'd be an all-day event, Erica felt trapped.

With nowhere to go and no one to spend her Sunday with, Erica ran upstairs to change her clothes. It was as good a time as any to go through her closet and weed out her clothes. Erica had, at most, a little more than three weeks before she left Pine for good and there was still a lot to do.

After sorting every stitch of clothing she owned into items to keep and thrift-store piles, she knew she'd kept too much, but it was a start. She scanned her bedroom. Two dressers and the king-size bed had been sold with the house, but she wanted to keep the pair of mission oak bedside tables from her mom. They were matching, small square-like stands with a drawer and cupboard. If they fit in her tiny-home loft, they could give her a little more storage and look nice to boot.

Emptying the contents of one bedside table, Erica found a medicine bottle that had been her late husband's. Seeing it hit her hard, making her slump to the floor. Bob had had high blood pressure and hadn't been the best at taking his meds. He'd been a doctor who knew the risks, yet he hadn't followed his own advice. Always busy looking out for others, but not himself.

"Oh, Bob," Erica whispered before she broke down and cried.

She thought about what Ben had said. He'd also known the risks of his job, but Erica imagined that seeing someone he'd cared about killed before his eyes obliterated any training or preparation he might have had.

Erica closed her eyes and prayed. She prayed for Ben and she prayed for herself, too. Her decision to sell Bob's house and take a traveling-nurse position had been a way to see the places she and Bob had longed to one day visit together.

Guilt gnawed at her for telling herself such a bold-faced lie. She wanted to escape from the memories of how relieved she'd been when heart failure had finally taken Bob from her care. Her late husband wouldn't want her feeling guilty. He'd hated the limitations he'd lived with as much as she had, probably more.

Ben's reaction to loss suddenly made complete sense to her. If he refused to feel, then hurt couldn't touch him. If she left Pine, then maybe she could outrun the memories that had held her hostage. She slipped Bob's medicine bottle into her pocket to toss in the recycle bin downstairs.

Lifting one of the emptied little side tables, Erica carried it awkwardly down the stairs and placed it in her tiny-home pile. That pile was getting bigger, too.

She headed back upstairs for the other one, when she heard the doorbell ring. Hurrying back down to answer the door, she first peeked out of the window and saw Ben and Atlas on the other side. Standing under the front overhang, Ben was wiping down Attie's back and paws with a towel. The dog sat patiently, not minding the attention.

Her heart beat faster as she threw open the door, both

glad and afraid that he'd come. "What are you doing here?"

"I came to help you pack or take stuff to your storage unit. I have my dad's covered truck."

"Wow, thanks." She stepped back. "Come in."

Atlas didn't hesitate to bound inside and circle her feet. He wanted pets and he wouldn't let her move until she complied.

"Hi, Attie." Erica kneeled down and loved on him. Even though Ben had dried off Atlas, his fur was still damp from the rainy drizzle and he smelled like wet grass.

"I hope you don't mind that I brought him. He needed a break from consoling my folks."

Looking at Ben's furrowed brow, she knew that he'd been the one who needed a break and her heart pinched. "Not at all. How are they?"

Ben shrugged. "Really broken up, but they'll be okay." He held out the towel. "Where would you like this?"

Erica took it from him and draped it over a chair, all while trying to get a handle on her feelings. He was here to help as any friend would. That was all this was. "I can show you what I have packed so far."

Ben grabbed her hand. "Are you okay?"

"Fine," she lied. Why was he always concerned about how she felt when he refused his own feelings?

"Erica, what's going on?"

She took the coward's way out. Instead of sharing the guilty feelings gnawing at her, she pulled out Bob's medicine bottle. "Sometimes it's the little things that hit hardest."

Ben looked at the bit of plastic, then cupped her cheek. "I'm sorry."

"Me, too."

Ben let his hand drop and gestured for her to lead on. "Let's see what you have."

Erica walked to the family room, where she had boxes lined up against the wall leading to the garage. There was quite a stack and a trip to the storage unit would really be helpful. "All this."

"Good amount." Ben nodded as he studied her stuff.

"If you back into the garage, we can load up dry and then we can back into the storage space and stay dry."

"Sounds like a plan. I'll do that now." Ben avoided making eye contact with her.

Erica ignored a stab of guilt for letting Ben think that she was only upset about Bob. She'd cried for him, too. And her.

She hadn't bothered pulling her car in when she got home and had parked in the turn-around spot closest to the front door. "I'll open the garage door."

"Attie, *blieb*," Ben said before he walked out.

Erica laughed when Atlas lay down at her feet, as if guarding her. Is that what *bleeb* meant? To guard? Or maybe play the chaperone. That thought made her chuckle, but then she was glad Ben's K-9 partner was here to protect her. Protect them.

She bent down to scratch behind the dog's ears. "You're a good boy, Atlas. You keep me and Ben in line, okay?"

Atlas gazed up at her with what looked like a smile on his face, almost as if he'd not only understood, but also promised to do just that.

Chapter Ten

After three trips to Erica's storage unit, Ben was glad he'd come. He should have texted her, but thought she might refuse the help she so clearly needed. The fact that she had a storage unit at all gave him some hope of her eventual return.

She'd saved a few furniture pieces they'd been able to take to storage, including her mother's hutch. He'd come back another time and help her load up the mound of stuff set aside for the thrift store, but those were mostly bags and manageable boxes.

When he pulled back into her driveway, the rain had stopped and the sun was playing peekaboo, hiding behind a cloud one moment, shining on them the next. Steam rose from the road and driveway when the sun stayed out long enough to heat the damp air.

Erica sat in the passenger seat with Attie stretched across her lap. The dog had sat between them all the way there and back. He wasn't quite sure what that was about, but his K-9 partner seemed to be guarding her.

"Thank you so much. That was a huge help. Do you want to come in for dinner? Nothing fancy, I was going to grill some chicken and veggies. It's the least I can do for your time." Erica shifted under the dog's weight.

Attie sat up.

Spending more time with her alone wasn't smart, but dinner sounded great. So against his better judgment, he shut off the engine. "Sure."

"Good." She looked both relieved and a little tense, but climbed out of the truck. "Come on, Attie."

Ben watched the dog follow her as he trailed them back to her house. Inside, he bent down to look over a really nice Mission-style table. "This is gorgeous. Are you keeping it?"

Erica turned to see what he was referring to. "I have another one upstairs. They were my mother's and I thought I'd use them in the loft of the tiny home."

He knew they'd look nice there. Not too tall, either. "Do you like this style?"

"I like old stuff. Always have."

Her place was pretty bare, even though there was still furniture inside. Plain furniture. No wonder she was leaving it behind. The nice antiques, she kept. There were no paintings or family pictures on the walls. He'd seen some in the storage unit, covered with moving blankets. Still, it didn't seem like Erica collected trinkets like his mom, or houseplants like Lori.

"Anything I can help with?" he asked.

"If you'd get the grill going, that would be great. It's on the deck through the family room slider." Erica was already at the kitchen sink, washing her hands.

"Will do." Ben turned to call Attie to go with him, but the dog followed Erica's every move, sticking close. Ben shook his head. Why he chose to watch over Erica was a mystery. A funny one.

Outside, Ben fired up the grill and waited for it to get hot before he used the grill brush on the grate. Standing on the decent-size deck, complete with a table and chairs set that he thought must stay with the house, Ben scanned the backyard. A thicket of trees separated her from her neighbor, but he could still see the log-style house beyond. Erica lived in a high-end subdivision, the only one in Pine. Even if her house was an older style, it still screamed of quality and being a doctor's residence.

"Do you like rice?" Erica stuck her head out the slider.

"Yeah." He wasn't a picky eater.

He grit his teeth. They'd made peace with their past last night at the fair, but it still irked Ben that she'd married Dr. Bob Laine. A man Erica still loved, given how wrecked she'd been after finding his old medication bottle. But Ben could never be like that guy, or measure up to the hero he must have been. Ben certainly couldn't afford a place like this.

He didn't want to compete with the memory of Erica's dead husband, so what did it matter? He wasn't out to win her over. He simply appreciated their friendship. Ben didn't have close friends. He didn't have close anyone, other than Attie. And his family, although, he kept them at a close distance.

He stepped back inside. "Anything else?"

"I don't think so." Erica looked up from slicing onions, peppers and zucchini. She drizzled olive oil on the veggies then dumped them in a grill basket and handed it to him. "You can put these on. I'll bring the chicken."

She had butterflied two chicken breasts that were marinated in something that smelled really good.

He walked back out with Erica following him and Attie following both of them.

"Will he be okay while we eat? Is he hungry, do you think?" Erica asked.

"He'll be fine." Ben would slip him a little chicken.

Again, Atlas sat between them while they loaded the grill.

"*Was ist los*, Attie?" Ben rubbed the dog's nose.

"What did you just say?"

Ben chuckled. "I asked him what is going on? He's sticking to you liked glue."

"Isn't *bleeb* a command to stand guard?"

Ben looked at her like she was being silly. "No. *Blieb* means stay."

Erica laughed then. "Then, I think he's playing chaperone." Ben let out a bark of quick laughter. "Why would he do that?"

"Because I asked him to." Erica turned to go back into the house and, sure enough, Attie followed her.

Ben's amusement faded. In the kitchen he asked her, "Were you worried?"

"No." Erica faced him. "Okay, maybe a little. When you brought him with you, I wondered if you were concerned about a repeat of last night on the Ferris wheel, so I told Attie to keep us in line."

Ben looked at Atlas.

The dog looked back.

Ben would kiss Erica with or without his partner's permission if it came to that. Ben would see to it that it didn't. Still, the dog had been listening to them, and Ben wondered just how much of the conversation Atlas really understood.

"I think we can keep ourselves in line, don't you?" Ben nearly laughed when he heard how it sounded. They were both middle-aged, not a couple of teenagers.

"Agreed. Now, can you go flip the chicken and toss those veggies while I make a salad?" Erica gave him a tight smile.

Was she having trouble keeping her distance? They were going in different directions and a romantic relationship would ruin everything if it didn't work out again between them. Just like when they were young, they both needed to figure a few things out.

Ben wasn't going to get in the way of Erica finding new purpose and healing from the death of her late husband. Nor would he let her too close so he'd feel the loss when she left. Nope. There'd be no kisses from him tonight, or any other night, because it'd be more about need and loneliness—two things that heaped a ton of regret if not careful.

With tongs in hand, he said, "I'll be right back."

"Do you want to eat in here, or out on the deck?"

Spotting a framed picture of Erica with Bob and her two daughters that was perched on an end table, Ben hesitated. They all looked happy in that photo. Erica's girls were young and cute, with their mouths full of braces. Dr. Bob looked distinguished and proud.

Ben pointed with the tongs. "Outside."

He didn't want to be reminded of her loss. Or his own. He was tired of losing people who meant a lot to him. Would God protect him, or would this newly found faith require him to surrender his emotions and feelings, and risk getting hurt all over again?

Wednesday morning, after two twelve-hour-shift days at the hospital, Erica was more than ready to see Ben. In fact, she could hardly wait to see him, and that wasn't a good thing. They'd had a nice dinner Sunday evening.

Ben had stayed and they'd hung out on her deck long into the evening, talking about everything she'd need for her tiny home. He'd also asked for the name of the volunteer coordinator at the hospital to find out more about the dog-therapy program she'd mentioned.

There'd been no good-night kisses when Ben left, or any talk about her guilt or the losses he'd suffered while a cop. Still, Erica was convinced he needed to work through the grief he'd never allowed himself to feel.

She arrived at the Fishers' with a flowering plant for Ben's mom. When she pulled in, Ben and Jason were standing outside enjoying cups of coffee in the morning sunshine. She parked and grabbed the plant pot, then set it in the shade cast by the side of the workshop.

"What's that?" Ben asked.

"A butterfly bush for your mom."

Jason smiled. "That was thoughtful of you."

Erica smiled back.

"Why'd you get her one of those?" Ben asked.

"In memory of Millie." Erica knew June liked flowers. She had a nice mix of both perennial and annual flower beds around the house, in addition to her vegetable garden. "I thought she could plant it in the flower bed out back, where Millie used to lay."

"She'll like that." But Ben's frown deepened.

She could tell he didn't want to revisit the memory of Millie's passing. She'd seen a quick flash of sadness before the frown. "What about you? Are you doing okay?"

"Yeah, sure. It's got nothing to do with me."

Sure it did. He'd loved Millie, too. She'd seen the tender way he'd carried her inside from out of the storm, so here was a prime example of detachment, as if he didn't want to mourn the loss. Or couldn't.

This wasn't the place to dig into what he was doing, or rather not doing, but Erica wasn't going to ignore the situation, either. She'd confront Ben about grieving when the time was right and help if she could. Changing the subject, she asked, "What are we working on today?"

"Your place."

Erica smiled. "Wonderful."

Ben slapped his son on the back. "Jason wants it done so he can devote more time to other projects, plus a new one he just contracted."

"Wow, Jason, you're tearing it up." Erica couldn't keep the pride out of her voice.

"Yeah. I'm finally gaining some momentum."

Ben offered her a cup of black coffee. "You must be close to leaving your position at the hospital."

"Tuesday is my last day, so three more shifts left to go." After twenty-seven years, she was trying something different. She knew the job she was heading for, but there was still a sense of the unknown waiting for her in Wyoming. It was thrilling but also scary.

Erica rubbed her forehead as that reality sank in.

"Nervous?"

Erica looked into Ben's eyes. "I'm a host of feelings and worries."

"What are you worried about? You'll do great."

Erica shrugged. "For starters, can I back up *The Wanderer*?"

Ben chuckled and the sound was warm and comforting. "I'll teach you."

"Thank you." It would mean more time together, but Erica desperately needed the instruction.

Jason had joined them and nodded toward her truck. "With that Super Duty, you'll be fine."

Ben noticed the truck. “Where’s your car?”

“Sold it.” Erica grinned. “For cash to a new RN at the hospital.

“Good for you.”

“Yup. Good for me.” Erica’s insides twisted. She wanted adventure, really she did, but her whole life had been in Pine. Everything familiar and safe. She might be nervous, but she wasn’t going to chicken out now. No way. “Hey, where’s Attie?”

Ben nodded toward the house. “He’s hanging out with my folks.”

“They probably need his comfort right now.” Erica was amazed by Atlas’s perception. Truly, a unique animal. He’d make a wonderful therapy dog.

“Yeah.” Ben downed the rest of his coffee in one gulp. “Ready to work?”

“Yes.” Erica took her cup with her as they made their way through the workshop and out the other opened garage door.

Every time she spotted her little gray cottage-on-wheels, she smiled. The outside was completed and it looked good, charming even. Stepping inside, she was blown away by how much had been done since she’d last been here. The walls were up and the white cupboards were all in place. It looked so pretty and fresh. Even her little woodstove had been installed.

“When?”

“Jason and I worked on it exclusively the last few days. It’s just you and I finishing up the interior. I hope you don’t regret going with a wood-burner instead of gas. You’ll have to find the wood and then keep it dry.”

Erica ran her fingers over the cast-iron stove that had

been set atop a slab of cut stone. "Nope. It has to be wood. There's nothing warmer."

She looked over the pine paneling inside. So pretty and light in tone—maybe she wouldn't whitewash it. It was nice as is. The living space didn't look big enough for a love seat, let alone a couch, but Erica wondered if a built-in bench might work.

She stepped over to just below the loft. "Ben, do you think we could build a bench for seating right here that would lead to the steps up to the loft?"

"Sure. I can do that, no problem." Ben rubbed his chin. "In fact, I have something that might work in my parents' barn. Would you like to take a look?"

"If it's anything like the bench you made your mom, then I'm all for it."

He nodded. "It's similar. Come on and I'll show you."

Erica followed Ben across the lawn, and into the two-story barn. It was smaller than most farm barns, but still had windows at either end of the top. The ground floor had a traditional barn door, as well as a regular-size door for access.

Once inside, Erica inhaled the scent of fresh hay and was transported back to when she and Ben were kids. She looked up at the second floor loft that had been built only on one side. When they were not quite teenagers, they used to jump from that loft into the loosened hay on the ground floor.

"Nothing has changed in here," she murmured.

"Remember when we used to jump into the hay?" Ben chuckled.

"I was just thinking about that." Erica followed him up the stairs to the second floor.

Ben walked to the edge of the loft and looked down. "We were reckless. That's a long way down."

Erica peeked over, too. "There used to be a lot more hay piled up back then."

"True. But it's a wonder neither one of us were hurt."

But they both had been. After she'd met Bob, she'd broken both their hearts. Erica brushed away that thought. They'd made peace with their past at the fair; it didn't do any good for her to hold on to it.

Ben walked to a corner of the loft, where he lifted a canvas tarp that covered a stack of furniture. Underneath were a couple of Adirondack-style chairs, a large chair made with an antique sewing machine bottom, a small table and a couple of benches like his mother's.

"You made all of these?" Erica asked.

Ben nodded. "Yeah, I did."

She ran her hand over the old cast-iron, sewing-machine-bottom chair. "This is amazing."

Ben smiled. "Thanks."

"What gave you the idea?"

"I found the bottom tossed by a creek while on patrol with my first K-9, Judge. I brought it home, but it sat for a long time. After he died, I figured I'd make a seat out of scraps from other projects. Then I made the back and arms."

"You could sell these, you know. Antique sewing-machine bottoms aren't that hard to find."

Ben shrugged. "I like that it's one of a kind, you know? Like Judge."

Seeing the pain in his eyes, Erica knew this was the time to see if she could get him to open up. "What happened?"

Ben ran a hand through his hair as if trying to sweep

away the memory, but, of course, he couldn't. Looking at her, he said simply, "He was stabbed by a perp he'd apprehended. Judge died in my arms."

Erica could have cried. All she could think of was Atlas in that same situation and it broke her heart. With a thick voice, she whispered, "I'm so sorry."

He pulled out one of the benches and sat down. "I've been told that I don't talk about it enough. Judge deserves better, but—"

She wondered if the police psychologist had told him that. Surely, they had protocols for the loss of a partner. Even a K-9. Maybe, especially a K-9. "But what?"

"It's easier not to."

Erica sat next to him. "The pain will always be there, but how sharp it feels depends on letting it all out. Vocalizing can help."

He looked cynical. "Is that what your grief support group taught you?"

"Yes." Erica prayed she said the right thing next. "I put away a lot of feelings after Bob's stroke. I had to, in order to care for him and get through the day. The relief I felt after he finally passed brought a lot of guilt I wasn't prepared for. I never thought I'd feel grateful for Bob's death. Pastor Parsons helped me with that."

"How? How'd he help?" He looked sincerely interested.

"I talked, he listened." Erica had cried and yelled, too. "I never felt judged for the feelings I shared, and some of them weren't pretty."

"Hmm."

"Give it some thought." She patted his knee. There was so much more to say, but should she push it? Yes, she should. "Ben, how did you handle Judge's death?"

"Not very well."

"Why?"

Ben looked right at her. "I shot the guy. He didn't make it."

Erica felt the blood drain from her face.

"Come on, we should get to work and you need to pick a bench."

How could he drop a bomb like that on her and then move on as if he could turn it all off? And that was exactly what he did. He shut down and didn't feel it. Didn't examine, or maybe he examined it too closely and that was why he appreciated hands-on work. It was no small wonder that Ben needed to keep his mind busy. He'd killed a man.

"What about this bench for *The Wanderer*?"

Erica looked at the piece of furniture he referenced. It was perfect. And she was trying to wrap her head around the fact that Ben Fisher, who couldn't shoot the coyote that terrorized his mom's chickens, had killed a man.

Without even thinking, she asked, "How much do you want for it?"

"You can have it." Ben wasn't about to charge her. He couldn't believe he'd told her what had happened to Judge and what he'd done in response.

Erica still looked shaken. She was struggling to act normal, too. "With a nice cushion, it'll be perfect in place of a couch."

Ben lifted it. "If you say so."

"Need help?"

"I got it." He lifted the bench with ease. Yes, he needed help, but not the kind she could give him. Nobody could. Maybe God?

Ben had been reading how God had wiped out whole groups of people in defense of the Israelites and some of it was pretty gruesome. God probably understood his angry response better than anyone.

After an administrative review by the department, his use of deadly force had been ruled appropriate under the circumstances. But Ben had taken that shot with a big dose of fury in addition to his training. He'd been taught to shoot center mass, but he lived with the knowledge that if only he'd have aimed differently, the guy might have lived.

As he carried the bench down the loft steps, neither one of them talked. He knew Erica was struggling with what he'd told her. She looked at him differently now and he couldn't blame her. It was probably better this way. They were getting too close.

He kept thinking about her taking care of her husband. He could read between the lines of what she hadn't said. She'd stopped being a wife and Bob, a husband. It had to have been a rough time for her. He couldn't blame her for feeling a sense of relief, or wanting to run from the memories wrapped up in the house she'd just sold. Her reasons for leaving Pine made sense. Her advice did, too.

Maybe he'd give Bill Parsons a call. Just to see if the pastor could shed some light on how Ben should approach God with all this. Talking hadn't helped with the department shrink, but then he'd been under a microscope. Saying the wrong thing, or *feeling* the wrong way, might have cost him his job. To this day, Ben wondered if he could have done something, anything differently. If only he'd been able to save Judge from that fatal blow.

They returned to Erica's tiny home, and Ben placed

the stout bench against the wall across from the woodstove. "How's that?"

Erica inched it over, but kept her distance from him. "I was thinking about the steps to the loft starting here. That way, I'd have a nice end table, too."

"I like it." Ben got busy taking measurements, and then he sketched out what he thought she wanted. Erica tweaked the bottom two steps, turning them to face the other wall.

They got to work building the steps, and by lunchtime, they were half-done. They'd kept conversation only to the work at hand, and Ben was pleased with how the steps were turning out. There'd be storage space, along with a safe way to the loft, especially after he added a handrail. He had a wrought-iron rail in mind, painted white. All he had to do was find it.

Jason peeked his head inside the open door. "Wow. This looks great. I like the stairs. You ready for lunch?"

"We are." Ben turned to Erica. "Mom is grilling burgers for lunch, so you're welcome to have one."

"Thank you. I think I will, but I have to get my plant." Erica left for the front of the workshop.

Jason spotted the bench. "Hey, one of yours."

"Yeah, I gave it to her."

"I want you know that I really like Erica," Jason said.

"What are you getting at?" But Ben had an idea.

His son shrugged. "You went to her church and found God, and you two seem really comfortable around each other. If you decide to pursue her for more than friends, I'm on board."

"Thanks, Jason, but let's leave that alone for now." Ben followed his son out the door.

He and Erica weren't happening. Especially now, after

he'd damaged Erica's view of him. *Comfortable?* That was a new one. Ben was anything but comfortable around Erica. She pulled things out of him he'd tried to keep buried. With her, he experienced memories and regrets mixed with a good dash of fear. Fear that he'd fall in love with her all over again.

This new faith thing was challenging, too. Everything he'd read in the Bible his mother had given him tested him. Pushed him to open himself up to not only feel, but also to forgive, and love. He'd blocked out all three for a long time.

He didn't want to love Erica only to lose her when she left. And even if he and Erica did get back together, would he pull away from her like he did with Lori? Opening himself up to love meant dealing with what he'd done and he wasn't sure he could go through all that again.

The scripture he'd read that very morning assured him that God was with him even if he walked through the shadow of death. And that was what he'd be doing, reliving the deaths of his partners, which had led to the death of his marriage. He had nothing good to offer Erica. Now, she knew that, too.

He spotted Erica giving his mother the plant she'd brought.

His mom hugged her and the two of them went right out to the flower bed beyond the deck. And Attie followed them. He watched as his mother ducked into the barn and came back out with a shovel. The two women planted that bush right where Millie used to lie, just like Erica had planned. They stood and stared at it. Atlas did, too. He sat right between Erica and his mom. An appropriate memorial if ever he'd seen one.

His dad brought out a large pitcher of lemonade and

set it on the picnic table that had been readied for lunch with plastic plates and tumblers. “What are they doing?”

“Planting a bush,” Ben said.

“What for?”

Ben chuckled at how much he’d sounded like his dad asking the very same thing this morning. “In memory of Millie.”

“Oh. Then, I better go and see.”

Jason poured himself a lemonade. “They sure miss that dog.”

“Yup.” Ben watched his parents and his chest tightened. Loss was never easy to handle.

Erica made her way back to the deck, but Atlas stayed with his parents.

“I thought I’d give them some space.” Erica’s voice was soft and her eyes were filled with unshed tears.

He poured lemonade into a couple of plastic tumblers and handed one to Erica. “Here.”

She took a long sip. “Mmm, best lemonade. Thanks.”

“Thank you for thinking of them.”

“Your parents are wonderful people.”

“Yeah, they are.” More and more, Ben knew coming home had been the right move.

Not only was he helping his son, but he’d also reconnected with his parents, which was long overdue. His folks had been thrilled when he’d told them about giving his life to God. Along with the Bible, his mom had given him a pamphlet with instructions on how to read through the entire book in a year—bouncing around instead of reading the first page through to the last. He was following that plan.

“You’re fortunate to have such a family,” Erica whispered.

"I am." It was something he once took lightly. Not anymore.

He had family around him, while Erica was alone. That bothered him. She belonged in Pine, but he understood her need to get away. The desire to make her part of his family hit him hard. He could see her so clearly here with them. With him.

But then how was he supposed to do that now that she knew?

Chapter Eleven

By the end of the day, Erica was happy with the progress she and Ben had made. Her storage steps to her loft were completed with the exception of a handrail, which Ben had gone in search of only moments ago.

Her tiny home was almost done. The appliances would soon be installed, hooked up and tested, which meant she wouldn't be working with Ben and Jason much longer. Despite the aches and pains of such hands-on work, she'd enjoyed her time here.

Seeing Ben regularly was almost over, too. Would she miss him? Yes. Was she falling in love with him all over again? Yes. Was she afraid of what he'd told her? Absolutely, yes.

All afternoon, she'd wanted to ask him for more information but realized that wasn't a good idea. She wasn't sure she wanted to know the gory details. Then again, she did.

Erica grabbed a broom and a dustpan from the workshop tool area and returned to sweep up the sawdust from cutting her steps. She wasn't sure what to do about her feelings for Ben. He'd already stated that they wouldn't work, and now she knew why. Sort of. Ben was the kind of man who'd be harder on himself than others. Obviously, he hadn't been terminated from the police force, so his actions must have been warranted.

Hearing his approach, she straightened and braced for impact.

"What do you think of this?" Ben had returned with a slanted length of an old iron hand railing.

"I like it. Will it fit?" Erica set aside the broom and backed up, giving Ben room to get around her.

He hoisted up the railing and held it in place for her to look over. The angle was nearly right even though the length was a little short.

"Looks good." Erica said.

He brought it back down and leaned it against the flat side of the steps. "It could use a coat of paint. White?"

"Definitely white. I can pick up some before I get here tomorrow."

"That'd be great." Ben stood in the middle of her living space as if unsure what to say or do. With his height and wide shoulders, he made the room seem even smaller.

She looked up at him. "Thank you."

He tipped his head, looking bemused. "For what?"

Erica touched the railing. "For this. Where'd you find it?"

"In my parents' barn. There's more pieces, so we'll get the fit right. Years ago, it used to be on their front porch."

"Oh, I can't take it. That railing belongs here."

His eyes narrowed. "It was in my dad's scrap-metal pile so, yes, you can take it. My folks would want you to have it. A little bit of their home for your new home."

That sounded exactly like something June might say and hearing it caused her to tear up.

Ben stepped closer. “What?”

Erica shook her head, trying to get control of her tightening throat. A teardrop rolled down her cheek, but she brushed it away, then managed a rough-sounding reply. “Leaving, and…oh, everything.”

“Scared?”

She nodded again, because her voice had left her.

Ben wrapped his arms around her and gently pulled her into a comforting hug. He held on loosely, as if not wanting to overstep, or worried it might turn into something other than comfort.

Erica stiffened slightly, worried about the same thing, but it felt so good to be simply held. She gave in and rested her cheek on his warm chest near his shoulder. She wrapped her arms around his lean midsection and her hands splayed against the solid planes of his back. There was nothing soft about Ben. His muscles felt hard beneath her fingers. Tense.

“Oh, Ben,” she whispered mournfully. She couldn’t erase the mental image of him holding a dying K-9 in his arms.

His arms tightened around her, drawing her closer. His spicy scent enveloped her, warming her even more. She didn’t want to move but knew she had to, especially when she heard someone outside, coming close.

Ben did, too. He dropped his arms from around her.

Erica stepped back, wiped at her eyes and turned to see a pretty blond girl with a surprised look on her face as she raised her hand to knock on the already open door.

“Molly,” Ben said.

“Hi, Dad. I hope I’m not interrupting anything.” The girl’s smile was wide, but her eyes narrowed possessively.

“Not at all. Erica, this is my daughter, Molly.”

Erica reached out her hand to the tall blonde. She resembled Ben some, but if Molly looked like her mother, then Ben's ex-wife was beautiful. "Hello. It's very nice to meet you."

Molly hesitated, but then accepted her handshake.

Ben ran his hand through his hair. "What are you doing here?"

"After your phone call, I wanted to come up and make sure you were okay."

Erica glanced at Ben.

"I told her about giving my life to God." Ben turned back to his daughter. "I'm good, Molly. Did you see Grandma and Grandpa?"

Erica noticed that Ben hadn't said he'd given his *heart* to God. Both were correct, and maybe she was nitpicking, but Erica had a hunch Ben was still holding out from complete surrender.

"Not yet. Jason told me where to find you," Molly explained.

Ben stepped out of the tiny home. "Well, let's go tell them you're here. Erica, I guess we're done here until tomorrow."

"Sounds good." Erica watched Ben drape his arm around his daughter and the two headed for the main house. She stayed put, feeling an odd mix of turmoil and shame. Ben's daughter had seen their embrace and she didn't look too happy about it.

Erica wasn't, either. She now felt empty with longing, not only for Ben's embrace, but also his affection. Before she could even think of accepting either, she needed to know what really happened when his first K-9 partner was killed.

Without that settled, there was no chance for anything deeper than friendship between them.

"Is she your new girlfriend?" Molly probed as they walked across the lawn from the workshop to his parents' house.

The late-afternoon sun beat down on them, hot and summerlike. Grasshoppers jumped with abandon. The nights were gradually turning chilly, announcing the end of summer was near. And Erica's departure for Wyoming was creeping closer, too.

"No. She's an old friend." Hopefully, their friendship would remain intact. Erica had been more than a little tentative in returning his hug. Until she'd clung to him at the very end. What might have happened had Molly not shown up?

"Jason said you were once engaged to her."

"Long before I met your mother, yes." Ben wanted his daughter to know that his feelings for Erica had nothing to do with Lori.

"Do you want her to be your girlfriend?" Molly's eyes had softened.

Ben looked at his daughter and let out a sigh. "What I want and what I should have don't always match up."

"Sounds like a girlfriend to me. Are you going to shut her out, like you did Mom?"

Molly had been only twelve at the time when he'd been under investigation for shooting the guy who'd killed Judge. She'd seen how it had affected him. She'd had big ears, too. Molly heard more than she should have at such a tender age. But then, Lori had always said too much. No wonder his kids hadn't been surprised by the divorce.

Ben tugged on his daughter's long blond hair. "What are you, family counselor now?"

Molly smiled. "No. I just don't want to see you hurt anymore."

Ben might as well have been punched in the gut, so unexpected was her perceptive comment that he'd been the injured one. "I'll be okay, Mol. Erica is moving away from Pine in a couple of weeks, so we're staying just friends. That's what it's got to be."

His daughter slipped her arm around his middle. "Okay, good. Now, tell me about this whole God thing you're into. Mom said you were serious."

He laughed and pulled Molly into a bear hug. "It's nice that you came up to find out. How long are you staying?"

"Through the weekend."

"Good. Then you can come to church with me on Sunday and see for yourself."

"Maybe I will."

"I'll hold you to it. Come on, let's go see what Grandma has planned for dinner."

"Attie!" Molly kneeled down as Atlas charged out the sliding door for her, yipping the whole way.

Nearly plowing her over, Atlas licked Molly's face.

"He missed you." Another casualty of the divorce. Both he and Attie didn't see Molly like they used to.

"I missed you, too, Attie." Molly stood after scratching behind the dog's ears.

"And I miss you," Ben whispered.

"I know." Molly smiled. "That's another reason I'm here. I miss my breakfast buddy."

Making breakfast for his kids had always been a weekend highlight. He missed that. "How is it, at home?" Ben could barely choke out the question.

Molly shrugged. "It's okay. I'm only there until the end of August. Then I head for law school in Lansing."

Ben grit his teeth. They could have waited until Molly was out of the house before Lori's boyfriend had moved in. His ex-wife had informed him of that when he'd called to tell her about his newly found faith in God. She'd been happy for him—whatever made him happy, is what she'd said.

Could he truly be happy, all things considered? He wasn't sure. He'd settle for contentment, but what he really wanted was peace. He wanted to make peace with what he'd done on the job and how it had affected those at home.

It hit him that Molly was finally going out on her own. "Do you need money?"

Molly laughed. "No. I have an apartment with a couple of roommates who are also attending Cooley. We're paid up through the end of the year."

"Have you met them?" Molly might be an adult of twenty-one, but she was still his little girl. Always would be.

"Yes, Dad. They're great. No deadbeats."

"Good. Just remind them your dad's a cop."

"A retired cop," Molly corrected.

"Right." Ben smiled and threw a ball for Attie.

Molly watched Atlas run into the field. "How are you two adjusting to retirement?"

"We're doing okay." Working with his son was great. Erica was part of that, but Ben really was enjoying himself, with the good, rugged, honest work. "I'm looking into certification for Atlas to become a therapy dog. We might volunteer at the hospital." He'd called the hospital contact Erica had given him and found out what he needed to do.

"That's great."

Attie grabbed the ball, but instead of bringing it back, he jogged for the henhouse. He circled it once to ensure the chickens were all inside the wire fencing.

"What's he doing now?" Molly asked.

"Making sure the hens are safe and sound." Ben wasn't certain what he'd expected for Attie, but his partner had been a natural at guarding the henhouse and comforting his parents. "Yeah, I think we'd both benefit from some volunteer work."

"Sounds like you're both doing well. I'm glad you're up here, enjoying all this." Molly spread her arms wide.

"It's nice to be back home."

Molly curled into him again as they took the steps of the deck and entered the kitchen through the slider.

"Look who I found," Ben said.

"Molly!" His mom hugged his daughter and then his dad did, as well. "This is a nice surprise."

"I can stay with Jason, if you don't have room."

His mom glanced his way. "Of course, there's room. Your father hasn't taken over all the guest rooms. Just one."

Molly grinned, looking like a little girl.

Having both his kids with him soothed like nothing else. His thoughts wandered to Erica all alone with her grown daughters so far away. He didn't like the uncomfortable pang those thoughts gave him, or the desire to fix that situation somehow. As if he could.

Later that night, Erica sat at the kitchen table with her laptop. She'd searched the internet for any information she could find about Ben's fatal shooting. Surely, there'd be a news report or something. Nothing but a professional profile popped up under Ben Fisher's name.

She moved on to the Grand Rapids Police Department's annual reports, starting with ten years ago and moved forward. She'd found a quick memorial for Judge in the K-9-unit section, stating that he'd died in the line of duty, but few details were listed.

She clicked into another year's report and found a blurb when Atlas joined the force to become Ben's new K-9 partner. There was a picture of the two of them, and Ben was smiling, but his smile didn't reach his eyes. Ben's hazel gaze reached out from the photo with a haunted glaze to it. It hadn't been but a few months after Judge's death.

There was no way his superiors would have kept Ben on the force if his use of deadly force hadn't been warranted. But Ben had made it sound as if he'd acted out of revenge. Had he? She wished she could find out more before asking him about it.

Erica had been stunned when he'd told her, so much so that she didn't want to accept it. For some reason, it had never crossed her mind that Ben might have killed someone. Noticing that he was different than the Ben she'd known made sense now. How could he not have changed after something like that?

This time she typed *K-9 stabbings* in her browser search bar and several articles popped up. With her finger poised on the mouse, she hesitated. Did she truly want to read about this? The fact that there were several results made her sick. The reality that K-9s were stabbed or shot for doing something they'd been trained to do tore at her sense of right and wrong. Was it right to put these amazing animals in harm's way?

Erica didn't have an answer.

As a floor nurse in a college town, she'd cared for a couple stabbing victims in her day. Stab wounds could be tricky to downright horrific. With those images in her mind, she scanned the results on screen for anything that might lead her to believe the article was about Ben's K-9.

And then she found it.

Grand Rapids Police K-9 Fatally Stabbed, Suspect Shot by Partner Later Dies from Injury

Erica clicked on the article and started reading. It might have been an episode from a police show on TV. Officers had been called to a home invasion, where a woman had been threatened with a bowie knife and assaulted. When the police arrived, the suspect had gone out the back door. Judge ran in pursuit, followed by his partner. Ben's name was not mentioned. She read further that after the K-9 apprehended the man, the man repeatedly stabbed Judge for release before the K-9's partner shot the man, who later died from his injury. The incident had been reported as under investigation.

Tears ran down Erica's cheeks. She couldn't stop seeing Atlas in Judge's place and she couldn't imagine what Ben had been going through in that moment. No wonder he didn't talk about it. The love between Ben and Attie was a tangible thing and she wouldn't believe that it had been any different with Judge.

Poor Ben.

Erica closed her eyes to pray, but she couldn't find the right words. All she could think to do was ask God to heal Ben.

Glancing at the time on the bottom of her computer,

she was floored by how late it was. Too late to call Ben. Even if it wasn't, what would she say?

She found herself praying for the right way to let Ben know that she'd read what had happened and she understood. No, that wasn't right, either. She didn't understand. She was furious that someone had stabbed a dog.

Erica couldn't set aside what she now knew and simply turn in for the night. She grabbed her phone. With fingers poised over the message button, her mind raced, but she hit the button and typed in Ben's name, then her text. Are you awake?

Waiting for his reply was agony.

No. What's up?

While trying to figure out how to text what she'd wanted, her phone rang. It was Ben.

"Hey."

"Are you okay?" he asked.

She swallowed the lump in her throat. She couldn't cry. That wouldn't do Ben any good.

"Erica?" He sounded concerned.

"I read about what happened to Judge online," she blurted.

No answer.

"Ben, I need you to know that."

"Why?"

She breathed. "Why did I look it up?"

"Yeah." His voice was low, like a whisper.

"You scared me by making it sound like you'd done something wrong. Ben, you didn't."

He sighed. "It's not that simple."

"I know." Erica choked up all over again. Of course, it

wasn't. She wished they were face-to-face, but it had been her impulsive choice to text him. She sniffed.

He was silent for a few moments. "Are you crying?"

"No." She was trying not to, but her voice sounded soggy and she sniffed again.

"Erica—" He stopped.

"I want to help, okay? If I can."

"I appreciate that." There was a smile in his voice.

"Okay." Erica smiled, too. "That's all I wanted to say." Not quite true. She wanted to say so much more—

"Good night, Erica. I'll see you tomorrow."

"Tomorrow." She disconnected.

Sitting there alone, she broke down and wept.

The next morning, Ben was in Erica's tiny home when he heard her sunny voice calling out "good morning" to Jason. He clenched his hands into fists and then relaxed them. Just how much did she know from what she'd read online?

He'd just finished installing the rest of the cast-iron railing that his dad had helped him cut and weld together. He stood back to check his work when she stepped in.

"That's perfect, thank you."

He turned toward her. "I'm glad you like it. I probably should have waited until after we painted it."

"No biggie." Erica lifted a brown paper bag from the Pine hardware store. "I brought the paint, so I can take care of that."

They were nearly done with *The Wanderer*. All that remained was some minor finish work and the installation of her appliances, which should arrive any day now. After that, there'd be no reason for her to continue working with them. No reason for her to linger in Pine.

Ben gazed at her, knowing they had some unfinished business from last night, but he wasn't up to it. Not today. Not with his kids nearby. "Erica, about last night."

She nodded, but remained silent.

"I'd like to take a rain check on that conversation."

"Sure." She reached out and touched his arm. "I get it."

Feeling the warmth of her hand on his skin, he was tempted to pull her close and drown in her hair, her scent, *her*. Instead, he stepped back. "I'll leave you to paint, then. I have to help Jason for a bit, and then I'll be back to finish up the trim and cap the outlets."

She nodded, but didn't say anything. Her eyes teared up and he worried she might cry.

His gut tightened as he realized he couldn't just walk out on her now. "Please don't."

She sniffed and quickly wiped at her face. "I'm sorry."

He was a heel, so he tugged her into his arms. "I'm sorry for hurting your feelings."

Erica held on tight. "You didn't. It's not about me. I can't stand what you went through."

She cried for him. Again.

Last night, she'd said she wanted to help. Could she? Erica had always had a way of stirring the deepest parts of him. It hurt too much to feel, but he could touch. Clutching her face between his palms, Ben bent close and kissed her.

He tasted the salt from her tears, but he wasn't gentle, like on the Ferris wheel. He kissed her with a desperate need to blot out the past. His and even hers. Theirs, too. He didn't want to think. He pulled the elastic thing from her ponytail and threaded his fingers through her hair, memorizing the heavy, silky feel of it.

Erica pulled back, her dark eyes wild. "Wow."

"Yeah." He couldn't help but smile at her reaction and reached for her again.

But she backed up, away from him. "You better go help your son."

"Right." Ben blew out his breath in an attempt to calm his racing pulse. "You okay?"

"Yes. I'm fine."

She didn't look fine. Her face was flushed and her lips were puffy. But she smiled and that was when he knew that he'd fallen in love with Erica Laine all over again.

"Okay. I'll be back in a bit." Ben stepped out into the August sunshine and rubbed the back of his neck. He'd been knocked completely off-kilter. Now what?

"Hey, Dad, you lost?" Jason called from near the twenty-footer under the pavilion. That tiny home was fast approaching its pickup date. The buyers had stopped in over the weekend and were anxious for it. They needed to finish that one up, too.

"Nope, just lost in thought." Ben hurried over. They needed to hang cabinets.

Jason laughed.

Ben hurried inside the tiny home and Molly was in there. "What are you doing?"

"Helping," she said.

Ben breathed a little easier. Neither of his kids had witnessed him with Erica. What had he been thinking, kissing her like that, right there with the door wide-open?

"Jason promised to knock off work after lunch, if I helped in here."

"What are you two planning to do?" One afternoon without Jason should be fine. Ben had lots to keep him occupied.

"All three of us and Attie," Molly corrected. "I thought

we could go to Au Train Beach and maybe get dinner afterward."

It was only a thirty-five-minute drive northeast of them. Ben didn't miss the fact that Molly hadn't included Erica, but then why would she after Ben had played down their relationship?

He looked at his son. "Is that a good idea with all that needs done?"

Jason grinned. "We'll be okay."

Ben ran his hand through his hair. Maybe getting away for the afternoon might be good. More like running away, but then he knew this could happen and he'd let it. He'd let himself fall in love. He'd gotten too close to Erica, knowing she would leave. He'd have to deal with that the only way he knew how. Bury the pain.

Ben looked at his kids waiting for his approval—he wouldn't let them down. "Sounds good."

"Yay," Molly chirped.

They got to work hanging cabinets while Molly nailed down trim in both lofts. By the time he returned to *The Wanderer*, it was nearly time for lunch. Stepping inside, he heard Erica moving around in her loft.

He went halfway up the stairs and spotted her capping off the outlets. She'd gathered her hair back up into a ponytail. *Too bad.* "Looks good."

"It does." Erica checked her watch and slid his way, no doubt to break for lunch.

Careful not to touch the wrought-iron railing that was tacky from painting, he backed his way down the steps and then outside.

She followed and closed the door behind her.

Once they stood in the sunshine, he finally told her.

"So, change in schedule. I'm taking the afternoon off with my kids."

"Oh, nice. That's good."

"We're headed for the beach." Jason had come up beside him. "Do you want to go with us?"

Ben inwardly cringed. He hadn't invited her.

Erica glanced at him and then at Molly, who had also joined them. She smiled, sunny as ever. "Thank you, Jason, but no. Not this time. You guys have fun."

"I'll go pack our stuff." Molly darted off.

"And I have to close up shop." Jason took off next.

Leaving Ben to face Erica. "I'm sorry, I just—"

"Stop." Erica briefly touched his lips with her fingertips. "It's fine. I have a million things to take care of at home."

He imagined that was true. "I'll see you Sunday at church then."

"Yes." She nodded. "Bye."

"Bye." Ben watched her climb into her truck. This time, he knew that he *had* hurt her feelings.

Chapter Twelve

Sunday morning in the church foyer, Erica had just filled her cup with coffee when she turned around and spotted Ben. He walked in with Jason and Molly on either side of him. They made an impressive sight, the three of them dressed in summery clothes. Ben and Jason were both wearing khakis and crisp shirts, while Molly had donned a pretty floral dress. She was a beautiful girl, tall and blonde. The family resemblance was strong when they smiled, which was exactly what they were doing.

Erica's heart swelled with pleasure at the way Jason and Molly smiled at their dad. They clearly admired him and Erica could see why. Ben was a good father and there was nothing distant or unfeeling in the way he treated his kids. He loved them dearly and it showed. But kids were safer than spouses, she supposed. Safer than her, too.

Ben saw her and nodded, and then he whispered something to his daughter.

Molly looked at her and waved. She pulled her brother into the sanctuary, when it appeared that Jason planned to follow after Ben.

It made Erica chuckle. Those pesky butterflies fluttered around in her belly as Ben approached and she had to remember to breathe. "Morning."

"Hi."

"How was the beach?" She hoped she didn't sound miffed that Ben hadn't wanted her to go. She wouldn't lie, his lack of inclusion had stung a little, but she understood that he wanted to be with his kids. Alone.

He gave her a crooked smile. "It was good. Attie had fun in the waves."

Erica smiled, then sipped from her cup. She wished she could have seen it.

"Sorry about not asking you to go with us."

She shook her head. "Don't be. You needed time with your kids."

"I did." He poured himself a cup of coffee and affixed a sip lid. "Your appliances came in yesterday. Jason and I will install them tomorrow. You'll be all set to haul *The Wanderer* home when you're done with your shift."

She'd be too tired after a twelve-hour day to go over how to hook up a tiny home. Jason would be, too, by the time she arrived. "Can I wait until Wednesday to pick it up? I still have to pay for it."

Ben smiled. "Of course."

She'd move some money around and then call his son to verify a good time to stop in. "And you promised me a lesson in backing it up."

"I did, yes." His gaze was locked on hers.

This felt terribly like a preface to *goodbye*. And she thought Ben looked a little sad. She was, too. "Well, I better go in and get a seat."

He stalled her with a soft touch on her arm. "Sit with us."

"Okay." She walked toward the sanctuary, aware of

Ben's hand at the small of her back. The warmth of his touch radiated through her, reminding her of the heat of his kiss only days ago. She wasn't going to kid herself—both felt nice. So very nice.

He let her slide in by Jason before sitting next to her.

"Morning," she said to both Jason and Molly.

They responded in kind and then the service started. The worship team invited all to stand and sing. When Erica stood, Ben did, too, and he slipped his hand into hers.

Oh, why'd he do that?

But Erica clung to his hand, knowing their days together were numbered. And Ben drove her up a wall with his alternating displays of affection and then pulling away from her. But then, she was the one leaving Pine. That had loomed between them from the start, and Ben had said that he didn't want a long-distance relationship. It was her fault for falling back in love with him.

Did she want a long-distance relationship?

Feeling the strength of his hand holding hers, she realized that she did. She wanted to at least give it a try and see where they went. What harm could there be in that?

A broken heart.

They'd been there, done that before, but they were older now and hopefully wiser. Ben had some issues he needed to work through and it might be better for him if she was gone to give him that space. Would he open up to their pastor, or simply fall back into locking his heart away?

She felt him lean close.

"Would you like to join us at my parents' house for dinner after service? My mom wanted me to ask."

Erica would love to, but did Ben want her there?

Gazing into his eyes, she realized that if he didn't, he wouldn't have asked. "Yes, thank you."

Ben joined in the song and his voice was deep and pleasant.

Erica sang along softly, but quickly glanced at Ben's kids. She saw Jason elbow his sister, then nod toward them. He'd noticed his father holding her hand and had pointed it out to Molly. Was the contact a positive sign of something more? Ben didn't try to hide their connection and surely he must know that his kids had noticed it. Maybe Ben might reconsider having a long-distance relationship. If she asked him, would he be willing to try?

Erica looked forward to dinner with nervous anticipation. She'd eaten with his folks and Jason before, but this was different. This was a sit-down Sunday dinner with both of Ben's children and his parents, as if testing the waters as a couple.

She was probably getting carried away with wish-filled thinking, but either way, she'd find out. After dinner, she planned to ask.

Ben leaned against the sink and watched Erica help his mom put dinner on the table. She chatted with Molly, who arranged the plates and silverware. Erica asked his daughter about her future plans with genuine interest and Molly reciprocated, asking Erica about hers. The two women spoke comfortably. His daughter had definitely warmed up to Erica and they moved around the kitchen with ease.

"Here, put this on, would you?" His mom handed him a basket of warm rolls.

"Sure." He set the basket on the table and took a seat on the bench he'd made so he could face the action going on around him. Atlas joined him and lay down near his feet.

Erica fit well with his family. She fit with him, too; she always had. He wanted her to stay, but knew she couldn't. Not only had she signed a legal contract as a traveling nurse, but leaving Pine was also important to her. She needed to go and see what was out there. And that was what worried him.

Would he lose her for good? Possibly. But he needed her return to Pine to be because she wanted to come back. It had to be her decision, not because he asked her to stay. And that was what made it so hard.

"Glen, Jason, time to eat," his mother called into the family room, where his dad and son were watching a Tigers baseball game.

His parents sat at either end of the table. Molly and Jason took the chairs opposite him, leaving Erica to slide onto the bench next to him. He caught a trace of her soft scent, which reminded him of the sweet smell of sunflowers that his mother cut and placed in a vase for the table. It suited her perfectly.

"Let's hold hands while we say grace," his dad announced from Erica's other side.

Everyone complied.

By now, Ben was used to holding Erica's hand, but it still brought him pleasure. It seemed natural to do so here, around his parents' table, where they had gathered as kids and then as adults. He bowed his head while his dad offered up a simple prayer of thanks and blessed the food. And then the bowls were passed around willy-nilly.

"Chicken, please." Jason reached for the platter loaded with grilled chicken slathered in his mom's homemade maple BBQ sauce.

"Potatoes." Molly was next.

"Wow." Erica chuckled.

He glanced at her empty plate, save a roll. This was different than their sandwich platters at lunchtime that were unhurried. "You have to be faster than that."

"Your family doesn't mess around."

"Nope." Ben and his brother had grown up competing for large portions at the dinner table, so they'd learned to move quickly when it came to mealtime. His son had followed in those footsteps and Molly wasn't shy when it came to food. "Your daughters didn't dig right in?"

Erica finally had the bowl of roasted potatoes in her hands. "Our dinner table was a very orderly affair."

He wasn't surprised. He'd always thought of her late husband as stuffy, simply because he'd been a doctor. Not that Ben had ever met the man, but he knew who he was. Bob Laine had been highly respected in Marquette. Pine, too. Everyone knew Dr. Bob Laine.

Ben offered Erica the next choice of chicken left on the platter. She chose a thigh and a wing. He took his fill, which made his plate complete, and dug in. He glanced back at Erica. She waited for the bowl of coleslaw. He chuckled when she reached for it, only to have his dad grab it first. But then his dad passed it to Erica with a sheepish smile.

On a beautiful summer day like this one, no one lingered long around the dinner table. Once finished, everyone helped clear the table and load the dishwasher. He turned to Erica, hoping for a moment alone. "Do you want to see your appliances?"

She nodded. "Please."

"Don't go far—I made a chocolate-cream pie for dessert, but we'll have that out on the deck," his mom said.

"We won't be long." Ben opened the slider for Erica to pass through first.

Atlas followed her out.

Ben grabbed a ball on his way and threw it for Attie. "I'm going to pursue what you suggested about Atlas becoming a therapy dog. I've got an appointment set up next weekend to start the certification process."

"Oh, Ben, that's wonderful."

"It might be good for both of us. We'll see." Ben was beginning to think his new purpose after retirement was not only helping his son's business grow, but also helping Atlas find his niche, as well. If they could do that together, all the better.

They walked silently the rest of the way across the vast lawn until they reached the workshop. Ben used his key to open the side door. "They're in here."

Erica followed him in. Attie, too.

"We usually install these before putting in the countertops, but this order was delayed for some reason." Ben had to say something. That little bit of awkward silence between them was killing him.

"I'm just glad they're here."

Of course she was. Erica had been itching to leave Pine for as long as he could remember. "Yeah."

Erica hunched down to examine them. "These look nice."

"Pretty basic two-burner stovetop, mini fridge and an all-in-one washer and dryer."

She rubbed her hand along the top of the washer-dryer combo. "This thing cost twelve hundred dollars, huh?"

Ben chuckled. "You'll be glad you have it."

"I'm sure I will." She looked up at him. "Thanks for showing me."

"Of course." He got lost in her eyes.

"Ben—" Erica clasped her hands together. She had something on her mind, something serious.

His stomach dropped. "Yeah?"

"Would you be interested in going with me? Just to drive *The Wanderer* out to Wyoming and maybe see a few attractions along the way. I'd pay for your return flight."

Tempting.

It was beyond tempting, but probably not wise. Definitely not wise. "Erica, I appreciate the offer, but my place is here. And I can't leave Jason right now. He's up to his ears in new orders."

She nodded and sighed. "I don't want to say goodbye to you."

He didn't, either. He tucked a strand of her hair behind her ear. "I know."

She tipped her head into his hand. "And you don't want to do a long-distance thing."

"No. And if you really thought about it, you wouldn't, either." He pulled his hand back and kicked at the ground.

They couldn't build a strong relationship starting out far away from each other. He'd wonder if she'd met someone new, someone more interesting than him, on her travels. It wasn't like it hadn't happened to him before.

She blew out her breath. "I suppose not."

He nodded toward the house. "Come on. My mom's got pie and we don't want to miss out."

"Okay." Erica looked miserable, but she managed to smile as they left the workshop. "I hope she made two."

Ben reached out his hand. "Let's find out."

Erica took it and held on tight as they darted across the lawn.

He laughed.

She did, too.

It was better than crying, but then she hadn't left yet, and Ben had a hunch that the worst of their goodbye was yet to come.

By the time Wednesday arrived, Erica was already drained after two emotional last days at the hospital. Her unit gave her a gorgeous bouquet of flowers and a hefty sum on a gas card, along with a farewell card signed by nearly everyone in the hospital. Her twenty-four-plus years as a floor nurse had come to an end, leaving her with a tumble of mixed feelings. She looked forward to the upcoming change. She looked forward to making new memories that didn't remind her of those last years with Bob.

From her to-do list, Erica had dropped off the last of her thrift-store donations this morning—check. She'd made arrangements with Jason to complete the purchase of her tiny home after lunch. He'd show her how to hook up everything and Ben would give her a lesson or two in backing it up. Another checkmark.

In a couple of days, she planned to have lunch with Ruth and Maddie one last time, and hopefully by then, she'd finish her packing and leave the next day. There was no reason to stay in Pine any longer. Her to-do list would be complete.

On her way to the Fishers' place, she knew saying goodbye to Ben was going to be tough. Really tough. After today, she'd probably not see him again. Everything that needed to be said had been said Sunday, except that he'd never told her his view of the events surrounding Judge's death. She may never hear it, but she hoped he shared it with someone, especially their pastor, Bill

Parsons. She prayed daily for Ben's healing from that trauma.

Pulling into the familiar drive, Erica experienced a sharp pinch to her heart. She was going to miss working with Ben and Jason. They'd shared skills with her that made her feel more empowered for this trip. Once she knew how to maneuver her tiny home, there'd be no stopping her. And that made her smile. It was what she'd wanted for so long.

She spotted Ben walking toward her, and again her heart twisted into a knot. Erica was missing him even before they'd said their final goodbyes.

Ben waved her over by her tiny home.

She followed his hand signal instructions to turn her truck around and back it up to *The Wanderer*. Once done, she opened the door, slid out of the truck and looked around. "Where's Attie?"

Ben chuckled. "I see where your priorities are. He's in the house for now. How was your last day at the hospital?"

"Emotional. I've been a senior floor nurse for a long time. Maybe too long." Definitely too long.

"Think you'll miss it?"

Erica shrugged. "I don't know. Maybe. I will miss some of the people I worked with, but it's time for a change."

Ben nodded.

Jason joined them. "Hey, Erica. If you'd like to inspect everything first, then we can go over the hookup instructions and finish up with payment and final paperwork."

"Great." Erica walked around to the back, where the door was located.

Under the pretty light fixture, there was a small, rectangular wood sign. The wood had been distressed to look old and the words *The Wanderer* were etched onto it in white, along with a scrolling-vine motif underneath.

She looked at Ben.

"I thought you needed the reminder." His hazel eyes didn't give much away.

She ran her fingers over the wood frame, feeling her throat catch and thicken. It was charming and perfect and a lovely gesture. "I love it. Thank you."

"Okay, okay, let's go inside." Jason rolled his eyes.

Erica vowed she wouldn't cry. Not in front of Ben's son. Not in front of Ben.

"I'll stay out here," Ben said.

It didn't take long to go through the inside and check over the appliances and the bathroom. From there, they stepped back outside and Jason showed her the water and electric hookups that worked like any RV. So far, everything made sense.

Then he showed her how to hook up *The Wanderer* to her truck's hitch, including a sway bar that he had special ordered for her. After plugging in the brake lights, they were ready to complete the paperwork for the title and registration, and she'd write him a check for the balance owed.

Erica glanced at Ben. "It's a lot to remember."

He gave her shoulder a squeeze. "You'll be fine. Jason has a pamphlet that will help. When you guys are done, I'll show you how to back it up."

She nodded, thinking she'd need more than a simple pamphlet, but followed Jason inside his little shop office. "Thanks for taking a personal check."

"No problem. I know it's good, and if it's not, I know where to find you. You gave us your new mailing address." Jason showed her the invoice. "You worked off a nice chunk, too."

Erica smiled. "Thank you for that. I'm so grateful it's all done. You have a great business here, Jason."

"Thanks. I'm glad we finished it early for you. I think we're going to do well. My dad enjoys the work, so now it's just a matter of making it grow."

It was work that Ben could hide in, but Erica understood. After signing everything, she gave Jason a big hug. "Take care and let me know how you are on occasion."

Jason laughed. "Sure will."

Erica left the workshop and met Ben at her truck.

He was all business. "Start it up and we'll make sure all the lights work."

Erica's nerves stretched tight. She could do this. She had to. This was the choice she'd made.

"If you'll take the passenger side, I'll show you what to do, and then you can try."

Erica scrambled over the console and waited while Ben climbed in behind the wheel.

"Here's a tip I learned. Turn with your hands at the bottom of the steering wheel, so that what's being towed will go where you turn it. If you use the top of the steering wheel, then the trailer will go in the opposite direction of where you turn."

She watched as he pulled forward slowly, then, using the side mirrors and his hand positions, he demonstrated what he'd just told her.

"Okay, your turn, and remember to use your side mirrors." Ben got out, came around the front of the truck and climbed into the passenger seat she'd exited.

Erica took a deep breath. "Okay, here goes."

She tried it, messed up and then tried again. The whole

time, Ben gently coaxed her, never once losing his patience. It took a few times, but she finally got it. Maybe not as straight as his example, but definitely doable.

And they were done.

"Good job," he said.

She gripped the wheel. "Thank you, for everything." Sucking in a calming breath, she looked at him. "I guess this is it, then?"

His jaw worked. "Not yet. Would you like me to drive with you to your place, just to make sure you're comfortable?"

Relief flooded her. "Yes. That would be great, if it won't put you too far behind."

"It'll be fine. I'll tell Jason." He slipped out of the truck.

Erica watched Ben jog back into the workshop. It didn't take long before he returned. When he opened the door, she asked, "Would you like to bring Attie with us?"

Ben smiled. "To chaperone?"

Erica let loose a nervous-sounding laugh. "No. I just thought it'd be nice, and I need to tell your parents goodbye."

"Come with me. I'll get Attie and you can say goodbye."

Erica hesitated a minute. "Should I leave the truck running?"

Ben shook his head. "You can shut it off. It's not going anywhere, but engage the parking brake to be on the safe side."

Erica did that and joined Ben as they walked to the house. Not hand in hand. Boy, did she long to hold his hand.

"I'm done for the day, so we can practice hitching and unhitching at your place. I'm sure you're going to want to use just the truck to bring me back home."

"That would be greatly appreciated. You're a lifesaver."

"Glad to be of help."

The small talk was one way to avoid the bigger issue of saying goodbye. Erica breathed deep. She'd tell Ben's parents goodbye now, but her farewell to Ben had been averted once again. She couldn't string it out much longer. Tonight was it. She'd say goodbye and be done with it. She'd also be done with Ben.

Chapter Thirteen

Ben had watched Erica say goodbye to his parents. She gave them broad smiles and big hugs, and his mom had surprised him by offering up their home if Erica ever needed a place to stay when visiting. Erica had looked surprised, too, and that resulted in another hug. He'd expected tears, but none came.

He'd coached Erica on pulling *The Wanderer* the whole way to her house. He'd had her pull into the driveway, back it out and then turn it around so she could back it up near her garage to park it for now. Then they unhooked the tiny home and hooked it back up to her truck to practice again. All this she'd done with a look of determination. She'd asked good questions and made no complaints when asked to do it again. And again, until Ben knew she'd be fine on her own.

With the truck freed from the tiny home, she looked up at him. "Thank you."

"Comfortable with it all?"

"Much more comfortable, yes."

There wasn't anything more to do but go home, only he didn't want to leave her just yet. He checked the time on his phone—late afternoon—but still early enough to do something together.

"Do you have to go? I can run you back—"

He shook his head. "No. I was just checking the time. Would you like to go for a walk? We could take that trail by the pond."

"Yes." Erica smiled. "I would *love* to go for a walk."

"Tense?"

"You have no idea." Erica looked back at her tiny home. "I was afraid I wouldn't be able to do this."

"But you did," Ben said.

"Yes, I did. Thanks in large part to your help. Want something to drink before we go?"

"I'll take some water." Ben pulled a small, squishy, red ball from his back pocket and tossed it for Attie to chase.

The dog scampered back for a repeat throw.

Erica ducked into the house and returned with a small cooler and a canvas bag draped over her arm. "Here, catch."

He caught the bottle of water she tossed his way.

Attie yipped.

"Would you like some, too?" Erica petted Attie's head, but looked up at him. "Does he need a bowl?"

"He can drink out of the bottle."

Erica pulled a cold bottle of water out of the cooler, twisted the cap and slowly poured the contents for Attie to lap up from the top. "He's really good at this."

"He's used to it." Ben had often given his K-9 partner bottled water purchased at a mini-mart when they'd run out from Attie's canteen bowl.

Ben opened the back cab door of Erica's truck for Atlas to climb in. She had a cotton throw on the seat that might get trashed. Ben could keep the dog from going in that pond, but he'd rather not have to. "Is this blanket a good one? Attie might get wet on our walk."

"It's old. He can lay on it." Erica lifted the canvas bag. "I have a couple of old towels, too, so no worries."

No worries.

He wished that he wouldn't worry about her as she trekked halfway across the country by herself. "Do you have your route planned?"

"Pretty much. I'm going to spend a few days with my daughter in Boulder, Colorado."

"Good." He'd kicked around the idea of staying in touch, but wasn't sure if he should. That would be too much like carrying on a long-distance thing. They should cut ties now and leave it at that.

They both climbed into the truck and took off for the trail. It was on the way to his parents' house, but definitely closer to Erica's. She pulled into the trailhead parking lot in mere minutes.

Erica slipped a water bottle into the baggy pocket of her shorts. "Want another one?"

"No. I'm good." The day was warm, but not overly so. Big white puffy clouds passed over the sun, making shadows on the path ahead.

Ben opened the back door for the dog. *"Hopp."*

Attie jumped down, but walked with them. He didn't run ahead. He didn't even ask for the ball to be thrown.

Ben guessed that Atlas knew Erica was leaving and didn't want to wander far from her. He knew how his partner felt. Of all the goodbyes he'd ever had to say, Ben dreaded this one most, not knowing if he'd see her again.

They walked silently, the three of them, for close to a mile before Ben cleared his throat. "I'd like to tell you about what happened that day with Judge, if you're willing to listen."

Erica's footsteps faltered slightly. "I am. Do you want to sit down?"

"No. It'd be easier if we kept walking." He'd promised to tell her, so he would.

"Okay." Erica slipped her hand into his.

He gave her hand a squeeze, but didn't let go. "You already know it was a home invasion, but it was called in as a domestic dispute. Judge and I were the second squad to arrive. Two officers were at the front door, while a woman screamed from inside. When Judge and I got out, I saw the assailant run from the back porch, so Judge and I went in pursuit."

Ben rubbed the back of his neck with his free hand.

"More backup had been called once it was known that this creep had a hunting knife the size of a small sword. Of course, Judge brought him down, but the scumbag refused to drop the knife. He stabbed Judge and I wasn't in range to use my Taser."

He felt Erica's fingers twitch, so he gave her hand another squeeze. This story was affecting her, too.

His throat grew thick. "I yelled over and over for him to drop the weapon, but by the third stab, Judge went limp. I drew my firearm and told him once again to drop that knife. Backup was running toward me on the other side, but they weren't in range to tase, either. The guy wouldn't stand down. He came at me and I fired."

Erica was quiet for a moment. "And the investigation found that the appropriate steps were followed."

"By the book for use of deadly force." Ben could see it all playing through his mind.

He always saw it. It may have happened a little over

eight years ago, but he never forgot a moment. He could still smell the wet ground and decaying fall leaves of the empty lot where it had happened. He'd never forget Judge's labored breathing before he finally died in his arms.

"Yet, you think you did wrong." Erica's voice coaxed him to explain.

Ben hadn't even told Lori this, and maybe that was the beginning of the end for them. He hadn't trusted her enough to understand. Maybe he hadn't loved her enough, either.

He needed to finally say this, share it with someone. "The guy had mental issues. I could see the frenzy in his eyes as I drew close, but then he went lucid and apologized before passing out. The trouble is that I *wanted* to kill him, Erica. That rage pumping through me is something I never want to feel again."

She stopped walking and reached for his other hand, making him stop, as well.

Atlas lay down on his feet with a soft whine.

Ben patted the dog, reassuring him. Then he faced Erica. Swallowing hard against the emotions clogging his throat, he added, "My biggest regret is that I didn't shoot sooner. I might have saved Judge, but I would have lost my job. To this day, I wrestle with that trade-off. I wrestle with killing that guy."

Tears ran down her cheeks as she drew him into her arms. "I'm so sorry, Ben. I don't begin to know what that was like, but I can understand how you'd feel the way you do."

He believed her and held on. "Going by the book cost me, but feeling too much cost me more."

Like now. Loving this woman and knowing he had to let her go.

* * *

Erica held on to Ben, her emotions raw and her voice thick as she prayed, "God, please heal this wound."

She felt his shoulders start to shake, and knowing that he'd been moved to tears tore her in two. She held him close, willing his heart to mend and the memories to fade.

She peeked around, noticing that they were the only ones on the path. Grateful for this moment of privacy, she gently rubbed Ben's back, offering comfort. She couldn't imagine that he'd want anyone to see him cry.

When he pulled back, he wiped his face with his hands. "Sorry, and thanks."

"I didn't do anything."

"You listened. And then prayed for me." He gave her a crooked grin. "Again."

"I pray for you a lot," she whispered.

Ben cupped her cheek. "Don't stop."

She wouldn't, even though they were going their separate ways. "I won't."

She held her breath when Ben leaned toward her, but he'd only been bending down to give Atlas a scratch. "Thanks, Attie."

The dog placed his paw on Ben's arm.

Erica took a mental picture of the image, tucking it away as a cherished memory. Atlas was a blessing to Ben and had no doubt helped Ben rally after Judge's death. But Erica was even more thankful that they'd both retired after hearing the harrowing tale. They'd bring others real comfort as a dog therapy team, wherever they decided to volunteer.

The question that hung on the tip of her tongue was why he decided to tell her now when they were saying goodbye. Was it because she was leaving that he felt safe sharing it with her?

"Shall we continue our walk?" Ben tossed the small ball up the path for Atlas to chase.

Attie brought it back and dropped it at Ben's feet for a repeat throw.

He obliged.

"Yes. We have yet to circle the pond," Erica said.

"Let's go."

So they walked on, chatting easily about the upcoming projects that Jason had lined up. Ben acted as if nothing had happened, as if he hadn't just broken down and cried.

"Ben?"

"Yeah?"

"Why'd you tell me what happened?"

He stopped walking and faced her. "You asked. Besides, after eight years of keeping silent on how I felt that day, I needed to tell it."

Erica nodded. Okay, simple. But it wasn't. Did Ben need more to process that trauma? Ben had asked her to keep praying for him. Maybe he knew what he needed to do, and maybe telling her had been the first step.

They continued walking.

"My parents gave me some land," Ben said after a bit.

"What will you do with it?"

"Maybe build or put up a prefab home. I already have the well and septic scheduled."

"So you're staying in Pine?"

"I am."

Erica found the news bittersweet and not a bit surprising considering the future Ben had with Jason's business. The two worked well together, and it also meant that Ben was putting down permanent roots. He hadn't been kidding when he'd said his place was here.

She playfully pushed at his shoulder. "You're not going to build yourself a tiny home?"

He chuckled. "I want a little more space and a big front porch."

"Sounds nice." She wondered what kind of home he might choose. He had a nice eye for the cottage style, but Erica pegged Ben as more of a cabin guy.

"You'll have to come see it when I'm done."

"Of course I will. And stay with your folks." Erica could imagine that visit all too clearly. The warmth of his family would feel like coming home. But it wasn't her home, or her family.

Ben fell silent as they reached the pond. Looking at her, he said, "Last chance to say no before Atlas goes in the water."

"It's fine. Really." Erica wouldn't dream of refusing Attie his fun. She had towels to dry him off, and a blanket for him to sit on. It wasn't a big deal.

Ben threw the ball into the water and Atlas went in after it, swimming back with it in his mouth.

"Bring," Ben commanded.

"Hey, that's English."

But Atlas came to her, dropping the ball by her foot.

"It is. He's getting a little big for his britches since retiring," Ben said with a laugh.

Erica picked up the ball, patted Attie's head and then threw it back into the pond for the dog to retrieve. They played like that for a while with Atlas alternating between her and Ben to throw the ball. The afternoon stretched into evening and Erica knew they were putting off the inevitable. It was time to say goodbye.

After Atlas finally lay down instead of chasing the ball, Erica turned to Ben. "I think he's done."

"Yeah, he'll sleep well tonight."

Would Ben? He'd dredged up some awful images in that short telling of what had happened to Judge. Maybe he'd finally found some sense of release. "Ready to go?"

He ran his hand through his hair. "Yeah."

They walked back to the truck. Atlas was nearly dry by the time they got there, but Ben still used one of her old towels to wipe him down before letting him climb in back. The short drive to his parents' house went too fast.

Erica pulled in and shut off the engine, turning to face Ben. "I guess this is it."

"Would you like to come in, and maybe stay for dinner?"

Erica shook her head. "No. That'll just prolong it."

"I know." Ben sighed and got out of the truck.

Erica did, too, then she opened the back door for Atlas. She crouched and gave the dog a hug, then kissed the top of his head. "Bye, Attie."

The dog stared up at Ben.

"It's okay, Attie. *Lauf.* You can go." Ben looked at her. "He wants to circle the henhouse."

Erica laughed as she watched Atlas take off toward June's chickens. "He's a good boy."

"The best." Ben rubbed the back of his neck. "I guess this is it, then."

"Yes." Erica took a deep breath. "I'm planning to leave Saturday morning, but I'll text you when I get to my daughter's. I'll let you know how I did pulling *The Wanderer.*"

Ben's hazel eyes looked dark, but clear. Actually, he

seemed clearer, too, as if a weight had been lifted from him. “I’d like that.”

“Thank you for trusting me with what happened to Judge.”

He shrugged. “You were right, I needed to tell it, but I wanted to share it with you first. I’ve got an appointment set up with Bill Parsons next week, so I’ll rehash the whole thing.”

He was moving on with his life, and Attie’s, and it sounded like they were both headed in the right direction. Erica touched his arm. “It’ll help.”

“That’s what I’m counting on.” Ben pulled her into his arms. “Goodbye, Erica.”

Erica buried her face in his shoulder and inhaled the warm and spicy scent of him mixed with fresh air. She forced herself not to cry. “Bye. Thank you for everything.”

He squeezed, then let go.

For a moment they simply stood gazing into each other’s eyes, and then Ben turned and walked toward the house. Atlas met him on the back deck and the two went inside through the slider.

Erica looked around, memorizing the pretty details of the Fisher place. The last few weeks she’d spent here had been good and she’d miss it. Taking a deep breath, Erica got back in her truck and drove home, letting the tears finally fall.

“Your tiny home is amazing!” Ruth Miller-Harris stepped out of the door, followed by Maddie Taylor.

“I love it,” Maddie added. “Thanks for having us over to see it.”

“Yeah, and thanks for lunch.” Ruth smiled.

Erica had ordered pizza and salad so they could have

lunch together at her place and then tour *The Wanderer* that she'd successfully hooked up to her truck all by herself. The last item on her to-do list could be checked off. "You're welcome."

"Erica, what you're doing is epic. Make sure you send us pictures along the way." Ruth ran her hand over the wooden sign Ben had made. "I love this, too. The perfect name for your tiny home."

"I think so." She was definitely ready to wander.

"So you leave in the morning?" Maddie asked.

"Yes. I'm going to stay overnight at a campground near Iowa City." She'd drive eight hours the first day, then twelve the next until she reached her daughter's place. At least that was the plan.

"Were you able to take everything you need?"

"Surprisingly, yes." Erica hadn't found the time to whitewash the walls like she'd originally thought to do, but that was okay. Had she done that, she would have wanted to show Ben and then they'd have to say goodbye all over again.

Ben.

It had only been two days since they'd taken that walk, but Erica missed him. While packing everything in tight and locking the cupboards for transit, she'd found herself wanting to ask him questions, or show him how she'd arranged the cushions on the bench he'd made. Everywhere she turned inside that tiny cottage-on-wheels, she saw Ben's handiwork. She saw Ben.

She thought of him constantly, but once again, Ben had cut their ties. This time, she was the one leaving the area, but just like long ago, Ben didn't try to fight for her. He didn't want a long-distance relationship, but then he hadn't even asked her to stay.

"Erica?"

Ruth's voice intruded on her thoughts. "Hmm?"

"How's Ben taking you leaving?"

Erica shrugged. "I guess you'll see at church."

Ruth and Maddie exchanged odd looks.

"He doesn't want to do the distance thing, so the timing just isn't right for us," Erica answered before they asked. "We're meant to be friends and that's it."

Ruth narrowed her eyes, then smiled. "Friends can be good."

Erica nodded. She'd wanted more, but really, what future could they have with her roaming around as a traveling nurse?

"Well, I'd better go relieve my mother-in-law from watching the boys," Ruth announced.

"Jackson and I are taking the girls to visit their grandparents in Escanaba, but we're hitting the beach there first."

"Sounds fun," Ruth added.

"Do you want to join us? It's only a forty-five-minute drive," Maddie said.

Ruth smiled. "You know what? Maybe we will. The boys would love it."

"The girls would love to see them. I think Zoe might have a crush on your Ethan."

"No crushes yet," Ruth said in mock horror.

They laughed.

"Okay, you two take off, but hugs first." Erica reached out to both women.

They shared a group hug, and Erica felt a sense of closure in leaving her friends. Ruth and Maddie had grown close because they had kids of similar ages in common. The two would continue to meet together, but not as grieving widows. They were each part of whole families now.

Erica felt the familiar twinge of envy. She had her daughters, but it wasn't the same as it used to be. Erica missed her life when Bob was vibrant and the girls were still at home. The family they'd been then was precious, but now gone. Never to return, but in bittersweet memories. It was time for Erica to move on and leave the past in Pine. She had new memories to make.

Chapter Fourteen

It was mid-November and Erica was lounging in her pajamas, sipping black coffee, while she wrote in the journal Ruth and Maddie had given her. Her day off had begun cold and windy with a rain-snow mix that made going outside a miserable experience.

She curled tighter on her cushioned bench and tucked a soft throw over her bare feet. While the wind howled, she stayed warm and toasty inside her tiny home with the fire that she'd built in the woodstove. She was so glad she'd gone with wood.

Erica kept her extra firewood dry in a covered bin outside, just off her steps, so it was an easy enough grab. She'd found a place in Jackson where she could buy smaller cut wood at a decent price, too, so she was doing well there. The year-round RV park where she lived was darling and the couple who ran it had made her feel very welcome. She loved it here, but she missed Pine.

Staring at the compact firewood rack she'd found at a flea market when visiting her daughter in Boulder, Erica was sorry she was going to miss spending Thanksgiving with her due to work. At least she'd stayed with Ashley for a few days on the drive out. They'd toured the Rocky Mountains together as well as every nook and cranny of Boulder. Erica understood why her daughter had no desire to live elsewhere. The area was stunningly beautiful.

Ashley had thought the tiny home was so cool that she'd wanted to look into building one for herself. Erica encouraged her to consider buying one from Jason, and her daughter promised to think about it. Erica had said she would help with the cost if Ashley went back to Pine for a tiny home. It'd be a fun visit for Erica, too. She wondered if Jason would let her and her daughter help build one together.

She'd see Ben if she went back. Would things be different between them? Erica shook off the familiar yearning for the man who still held her heart. She hadn't heard a peep out of him in two months. He'd obviously moved on without her. She hadn't reached out, either, so maybe he thought the same thing about her.

Erica scanned the photos of where she'd been since leaving Michigan. The drive out had been focused, but Erica still managed to take pictures every time she stopped for gas or a break. Colorado and visiting Yellowstone National Park and the Grand Teton National Park had all been exciting and filled with photo taking. The mountains were gorgeous, and she even had some great views from her RV spot, but she missed Pine.

"My mail!" Erica slapped her forehead. She'd picked it up from the post office yesterday, stuffed it in her purse and forgotten about it.

Before leaving Pine, she'd set up her mail to be forwarded to a post office box in Jackson, Wyoming, that she'd reserved and paid for online. She didn't get a lot of snail mail, as her bills were sent electronically, but she didn't want to ever miss the occasional card from Ruth or Maddie or friends from work and church.

She flipped through the small stack that consisted of a greeting card, a magazine subscription request and a local advertisement. She stopped when she spotted Ben's name on an envelope.

Finally, something.

With heart pounding, she tore through the envelope and pulled out a letter. Ben had written her a letter!

Unfolding the page, she read with greed.

Erica,

I thought it would be easier to write than text you. All is well here. The weather has turned cold and snowy. We got at least ten inches last night. Jason's tiny-home business has slowed down, which allows more time for Attie and me to volunteer at a hospice house this side of Marquette. Erica, you would be so proud of him. Atlas brings joy to the folks there and a sense of home. Families have said how much having Attie there means to them. Spending time with these people helps me, too.

One of the men there is an Iraq-war veteran, so we've shared some common ground. Attie doesn't want to chase the ball as much as he used to, which worries me, but the vet says he's in prime shape, so it's not health-related. I don't know, maybe he's fulfilled and has grown a little lazy. The chickens stay inside the coop these days, but Attie still checks on them. I've been meeting regularly with Pastor Bill Parsons. I'm finally making peace with my past. God is good. He answers prayer and mends the broken places. I guess you could say that I'm fulfilled, too.

My folks say hello and so does Jason. Attie misses you.

I do, too.

Ben

Erica reread the letter, cherishing every word. She'd been praying for him and God certainly had answered her prayers. Ben was healing.

He wrote well, even if his penmanship was a little rough. Oh, how she wanted to call him and tell him how much she'd missed him. She loved him, too, but was he ready for that? He'd written that he was fulfilled. That sounded like ready to her.

Picking up her phone, she hesitated and then decided against it. He hadn't called her. He hadn't exactly professed any feelings for her, either. Other than missing her…

Pulling a couple sheets of paper from a nearby drawer, Erica followed Ben's lead and wrote a letter of her own.

Dear Ben,

I have about four weeks left on my first traveling-nurse contract. The position I am filling in for is on an ICU floor and I find myself drawn to the critical and terminally ill patients and their families, so I know exactly what you mean about sitting with people in hospice. Caring for Bob all that time must have prepared me for the needs and questions here. I can't quite explain it, but I think I've found renewed purpose right here, where I least expected it.

And you're right, I am proud of Attie. And you, too. Tell him I miss him and give him a kiss from me.

The RV park where I'm staying is amazing and *The Wanderer* is just perfect. I'm warm and comfortable with everything I need. You were right again! The washer-dryer combo was a must-have.

I've included some pictures, so you'll see what I mean about the beauty out here. The views of the mountains are stunning. But I miss Pine. And I miss you, too.

Erica

She folded the letter and placed it in an envelope, but didn't seal it. She'd take some pictures, get them printed and pop a few in for Ben. Maybe, when he saw the pictures, he might call, and then she'd know for sure. She'd love to hear his voice.

He missed her!

Erica grinned as that reality washed over her. Maybe she hadn't read between the lines deep enough and this was all the sign she needed. She'd been toying with the idea of returning to Pine and had looked up nursing positions that were available. She'd even considered going back to the hospital, but she'd waited until she knew.

Feeling an overwhelming sense of peace, Erica now knew it was time to make a real plan, one that would serve them all well. Even Attie. Hearing about Atlas's newfound purpose seemed to fall right in line with hers.

After slipping the wedding band off from her finger, Erica went up her steps to the loft and dropped the ring into her little jewelry box. It was time to view the sorrow-filled memories of her past as preparation for her future.

And, if she could make it all come together like she hoped, she'd need room for someone else's ring on her finger.

Ben took a walk to check the progress on the foundation for the modular home he'd ordered. The snow had slowed things a little, but not much. The basement was looking good and would soon be ready for his chalet-style home to be set and the deck built. He hoped to be moved in by Christmas.

He threw the ball for Attie, but his K-9 partner retrieved it only a couple of times and then quit. Either the dog had recently decided that he didn't like chasing after a ball in the snow, or he simply didn't feel the need to do it quite so much as before.

"Come on, Attie, let's go check the mailbox."

Attie perked up as they walked toward the road. Ben hoped to find a return letter from Erica. It had been well over a week since he'd mailed his. He'd received no text or phone call, but then, he hadn't followed up to make sure she'd gotten his letter, either.

He liked to think he knew Erica, and he was pretty sure she'd write him back. Still, if he didn't see something from her soon, he'd break down and call her. He could always use wishing her a nice Thanksgiving as his excuse. It had been tricky not calling her, but he didn't trust himself not to beg her to come back. He missed her something fierce and that missing had only grown worse as the weeks passed.

Grabbing the stack of mail, he flipped through it and smiled when he spotted an envelope from Erica. "Come on, Attie, let's go inside and read what she has to say."

Atlas followed as Ben stepped into the house. Jason was reclining by a roaring fire in the hearth and enjoying a plate of chocolate-chip cookies straight from the oven. The whole house smelled good, but Ben was laser-focused on the letter. He'd have cookies later.

Attie trotted over by Jason and lay down by the fire.

"Here's the mail, Mom," Ben called out before pouring himself a cup of coffee. He sat down at the table and opened Erica's letter.

A few photos fell onto the table, so he spread them out. He perused pictures of the mountains, one of *The Wanderer* with mountains in the background and one of Erica next to her tiny home, pointing at a bin filled with firewood.

The last one made him laugh. And his heart twisted with homesickness. He missed her even more now, seeing her in that photo with a cheeky expression. He could hear her telling him that wood was so much better.

"What's so funny?" Jason asked.

"Erica and her firewood. She sent me a letter with pictures."

Jason came near to look at the photos. "Wow, it's beautiful there."

"It is." Ben started reading the letter.

"What does she have to say? Does she like it out there?"

Ben's heart sank. She missed Pine and she missed him, but she'd found renewed purpose in her career right there in the ICU. It sounded too much like she planned on staying.

"She's doing great," Ben said. "The tiny home is working out well, too."

"Cool."

"Yeah." But it wasn't cool. Not at all. It didn't sound like Erica was ever coming home.

His mom picked up a photo. "Oh, these are great. Erica looks good, too."

"She does." More than good, she looked beautiful and *happy*. He stared at that photo of her, willing her to come home. But it might be a lost cause.

His mom rubbed his shoulder. "Did you tell her how much you miss her? We all do."

"Yes, Mom. I sure did." Ben folded up the letter and stuck it in his back pocket. The photos he left on the table. Grabbing a cookie, he headed for the door. "I'll be in the workshop finishing up those cupboards."

"I'll be right there." Jason had helped himself to more coffee and was standing by the sink drinking it.

Atlas, the smart dog, was stretched out near the fire.

Ben gave his mom a hug. "Thanks for the cookies."

"Maybe you should visit her."

He shrugged. "Not until after my house is done."

"But she might have moved on by then, on to another assignment."

"It sounds like she's staying right where she's at, so maybe I'll visit her for Christmas." He didn't want her spending the holiday alone.

Although her oldest was within a day's drive, so she might be headed there. They could meet in Boulder, he supposed, but then he slammed the brakes on those thoughts.

Before he made any plans to hop on the next plane, he needed to seriously consider his options. He didn't want to spend his life without Erica, yet he didn't want a long-distance relationship, either. So either he had to convince her to come back to Pine, or be willing to move out there.

Gritting his teeth, he considered the house he was putting in. Had he jumped the gun on all that? Didn't matter. It'd make a nice vacation spot or real retirement home if he ended up leaving. Jason could live there for now, if he wanted to. One thing Ben knew for sure was that he was over living apart from the woman he loved.

One way or another, he'd start the upcoming New Year with Erica at his side.

Two weeks before Christmas, Erica turned into the Fishers' driveway and smiled. June had Christmas wreaths with big red bows hanging everywhere. It was a pretty sight that made Erica feel like she was home. Pine had always been her hometown, but this past summer, the Fishers had become her family. Surely, they would welcome her back. She'd counted on it.

There was a good amount of snow, but the drive had been plowed, as had a large area near the Superior Tiny Home workshop. She pulled in there, shut off the engine and got out.

Hearing a yip, she spotted Atlas running for her. He plowed through the snow and she kneeled down to hug the dog when he finally came near.

"Hi, Attie!" Erica buried her face in his soft fur, then looked up to see that Ben wasn't far behind.

The expression on his face was worth the agony of not telling him she was coming home. They'd exchanged more letters, but had never once called each other. It had been a fun way to connect even though they'd tiptoed around their feelings. Never writing it out in words.

Ben ran toward her, breathing heavily when he finally stopped. "What are you doing here?"

She stood and threw her arms open wide. "Merry Christmas!"

He grabbed her and pulled her close. "Merry Christmas."

And then he kissed her.

Erica kissed him back with abandon. This had definitely been the right move. Maybe even the right way to go about it, too. Ben's kiss told her everything she needed to know.

He finally pulled away, but not before rubbing his cold nose against hers. "How long are you home for?"

She grinned. "Forever."

He looked visibly moved. "Man, am I glad to hear you say that."

"Why?" She tipped her head.

He grabbed her mitten-covered hand. "Come see."

She walked with him along a snow-blown path that wound quite a way beyond the workshop. A lovely chalet-style home had been positioned into a small rise in the land, allowing for a walk-out basement. She could see a plowed driveway on the other side of the peaked roof that faced south. There were two huge windows above two large sliders that led to a wraparound deck. The place was not only beautiful, but was also brand-new.

"Yours?"

"Yes. Just completed. Come on in." Ben opened the door for her.

"Wow. You weren't kidding about the big porch." She went inside and kicked off her boots.

The interior was warm, so she shrugged out of her coat, hat and mittens. There wasn't any furniture, or anything, anywhere. "You haven't moved in yet."

"Not yet, but soon." Ben took off his coat and boots, too. "I just finished painting, but come on, I'll give you the tour."

Erica loved how open and spacious it was, even though the size was fairly modest. The living room merged into an open kitchen and a huge floor-to-ceiling stone fireplace was nestled between those huge windows and sliding glass doors. "Wow. That is stunning."

He grinned. "I splurged on the fireplace. There's three bedrooms and two baths. The main bedroom is upstairs. Come on."

Attie darted up the stairs first, then danced around at the top, waiting for them.

"He seems to like it," Erica said.

"I think so."

Erica loved the loft view of that grand fireplace. "Ben, this is so nice and cozy. How'd you do all this so quickly?"

"It's a prefabricated modular." He opened the door to the bedroom, painted a soft sage-green.

It reminded her of the day she'd recommended a sage tile backsplash. Looking around, she smiled. It was definitely a large room with a full bath beyond.

"Well, what do you think? Could you live here?"

Erica let loose a nervous laugh. "But it's yours."

"I want it to be ours."

Her breath caught when Ben went down on his knee.

"Marry me, Erica."

"And you're getting right to it, aren't you?" Her pulse was racing. This was exactly what she'd hoped for and counted on when coming home.

He grinned up at her. "Why beat around the bush? I was ready to pack up and move to Jackson after I got your first letter. I thought you were staying there."

Erica kneeled, too. "Why would you think that?"

"You said you'd found renewed purpose in the ICU."

She brushed back a fringe of his hair that had fallen across his forehead. "I did, but I found the job *here*. I'm starting as an RN case manager at the very hospice-care facility where you and Attie volunteer. If you'll agree,

Attie can go with me as either a full- or part-time therapy dog. The director already loves him, and I think knowing Atlas is what got me the job."

"Atlas would love it. I can go over training commands with you, too. I'll still volunteer, but I can go with you both at first, whatever it takes." Ben took her left hand and rubbed her third finger. Noticing it was empty, he quickly looked up. "When did you take off your ring?"

"After I read *your* first letter." Erica smiled. "That's when I reached out to hospice back here. They had an opening, and after a couple online interviews, I was hired."

"And you never called to tell me any of this." Ben squeezed her hand. "It would have relieved a lot of angst, you know."

Erica gave him a sheepish smile. "I wanted to surprise you. You know, like a Christmas gift."

He shook his head. "Best gift ever. So are you going to answer my question?"

Erica laughed. Had he even asked? More like demanded, but she was okay with that. More than okay. "Yes, Ben. I will marry you, because I love you."

"I love you, too." He kissed her, quick and hard.

Just when Erica tried to deepen their kiss, she felt Atlas nudge between them. "What?"

Attie licked her face.

She laughed.

"He really missed you."

Erica scratched behind the dog's ears. "I missed you, too, Attie."

Ben stood and helped her to her feet. "Are you hungry? Dinner's not for a bit yet."

Erica shook her head. "I'm fine."

"Tired?"

"A little, but I can always nap later. I was hoping to stay here tonight, in *The Wanderer*, before checking out a couple of places near Marquette. Did you know there's a year-round RV park off Route 28?"

Ben shook his head. "You'll stay right here."

She scrunched her nose. "Where would I plug in?"

"Right here, or you could plug into the workshop. It'd be good advertising. You could also move into our house and I can remain with my folks until we get married."

Erica loved how Ben referred to his new place as *theirs*. A tangible sign that he wasn't holding anything back from her. "With that fireplace, sounds like a dream come true."

"Consider it yours." Ben wrapped his arm around her. "Let's go tell the family. I'm sure they've seen your truck and are wondering."

"In a minute." Erica turned so she could look him in the eyes. "Ben, I want you to know that I love you even more now than I did before. Does that make sense?"

"It makes perfect sense. We have God in common now and this time around we're going to place our trust in Him. I've always loved you, Erica, but I finally feel like I can offer you a whole heart and I'm not afraid to let you inside it."

Erica felt her eyes tear up. "That's a real dream come true."

"God answered your prayers and I am forever grateful." He kissed her forehead.

"I can't wait to tell your family."

"They're your family, too," Ben whispered.

"They are, aren't they?" Erica's heart nearly burst.

God had not only brought her home, but He'd also blessed her with a second chance at love and fulfillment and a whole family to share it with. She'd never be alone again.

Epilogue

Christmas morning, Erica had never felt more blessed as she gazed at her husband, Ben. *Her husband!*

He was making a huge breakfast for all of them while she handed out the gifts to his kids and hers. The savory aroma of fried sausage filled their home, along with the occasional whiff of their freshly cut Christmas tree decorated only with white lights. Erica had no clue where she'd put her Christmas ornaments in storage and had given up searching.

"How's it look?" she asked Ben.

"Time enough to open presents while the biscuits bake." He came around the island to sit on the floor next to Attie.

The dog rolled onto his lap for a belly rub.

Erica's two daughters and Ben's two kids tore through Christmas wrapping paper while June and Glen looked on. Erica could barely keep it together, waiting for Ben to give his parents their present. Her heart was full, surrounded by family. It was a Christmas filled with love and laughter. The very best kind.

She and Ben had been married the night before, during the Christmas Eve service at church. It had been a quick yet perfect ceremony she'd always cherish. Erica had worn a simple red velvet dress she'd had for ages and her daughters and Molly had made a beautiful bouquet of white roses, white poinsettias and pine. That bouquet now graced their dining room table as a centerpiece.

They'd even made a boutonniere for Ben, who had looked so handsome in a black suit. After the service, they'd enjoyed a light reception with hors d'oeuvres at Ben's parents' house. No one had stayed long, and both Maddie and Ruth had come with their husbands. Erica and Ben had then spent their wedding night in their new home while her girls and Molly stayed with June and Glen, and Jason stayed at his own place.

Her daughters, Ashley and Emily, got along well with Molly and Jason. Although Ben's son teased her girls something awful, both daughters took it in stride and teased him back. Erica was grateful to Jason for making the mixing of their families a little more fun. They were all together and that was what was important. This was what Erica had missed for so long, and she enjoyed every moment.

Once their kids had finished, she glanced again at Ben. "Ready?"

"Ready." Ben got up and went downstairs.

All eyes were on his parents when Ben returned with a sleepy, blond bundle of fluff. He handed his parents a very sweet golden retriever puppy. "Mom, Dad. Merry Christmas."

June looked at her and then up at Ben, as she took the puppy from him and looked the little guy over. "Oh, my. What's his name?"

"That's for you to decide." Ben smiled.

His dad patted the puppy. "He's lighter in color than Millie was at this age."

Attie nudged the puppy, then dropped down into a playful bow.

The puppy paid no attention to Attie. He yawned and then curled into June's lap. And Erica watched her mother-in-law melt before her eyes.

"I think we should call him Marshall. He's soft like a big marshmallow."

"Marshall, it is," Glen said.

Everyone laughed and the puppy perked up.

Attie sat down and tipped his head, but his attention stayed focused on that puppy.

Ben scratched behind Atlas's ears. *"So ist Brav."*

Erica knew that was a term of praise, and she looked at Ben, who held her gaze. They had reason to give lots of praise. They were finally at peace with their lives. She thanked God for bringing them back together and giving them a home filled with renewed purpose and joy.

And sweet dogs to love.

* * * * *

If you enjoyed this K-9 Companions book,
be sure to look for
Their Inseparable Bond
by Jill Weatherholt,
available in February, wherever
Love Inspired books are sold!

And pick up these previous titles in Jenna Mindel's
Second Chance Blessings miniseries:

A Secret Christmas Family
The Nanny Next Door

Available now from Love Inspired!

Dear Reader,

Thank you for picking up Erica Laine's story of her second-chance blessing with Ben Fisher. I hope you enjoyed their journey to restoration through God's grace. I enjoyed writing characters that were a little older with more of life's battle scars. Erica and Ben had a long history, so I was happy to bring them back together and finally make peace with their past.

I am also honored to be part of the K-9 Companions Love Inspired series because I adore dogs! Atlas, Ben's K-9 partner, grew out of online research. But as I wrote, Attie took over and became very real to me. Hopefully, he came to life for you, as well. My husband and I have always had dogs, and we've been blessed by the many that have made their way to us. They're intuitive creatures. They know if I'm upset and give comfort. Our first beagle never left my side whenever I was sick. Our rat terrier, Peanut, understands just about everything I say—seriously.

It is no surprise how valuable therapy dogs and K-9 partners from all occupations can be. My heart breaks for those who've fallen in the line of duty, but the success stories outweigh the sad. So hug your pets, for they truly are gifts from above, and may God bless you!

I'd love to hear from you. Feel free to drop a note in the mail to PO Box 2075, Petoskey, MI 49770, or check out my website, which has a newsletter sign-up at www.jennamindel.com.

Or follow me at Facebook.com/authorjennamindel.

Jenna

COMING NEXT MONTH FROM
Love Inspired

THE WIDOW'S BACHELOR BARGAIN
Brides of Lost Creek • by Marta Perry

When her sons discover a teenage girl sleeping in the barn, Amish widow Dorcas Bitler finds herself caught between the rebellious runaway and Jacob Unger, the girl's stubborn uncle. Dorcas is determined to mend their relationship...but falling for Jacob was never part of the plan.

THEIR FORBIDDEN AMISH MATCH
by Lucy Bayer

Hoping to meet the brother he's never known, doctor Todd Barrett arrives in Hickory Hollow, Ohio, full of hope—but immediately clashes with local Amish midwife Lena Hochstetler. They don't seem to agree on anything...until they discover deeper feelings that just might complicate both their lives.

THEIR INSEPARABLE BOND
K-9 Companions • by Jill Weatherholt

Olivia Hart has one goal: to convince her ailing grandmother to move to Florida with her. The last thing she expects is for service dog trainer and single dad Jake Beckett to change *her* mind. Will a rambunctious puppy and twins bring two reluctant hearts together?

A VALENTINE'S DAY RETURN
Sunset Ridge • by Brenda Minton

Ending his marriage to his childhood sweetheart was the biggest mistake Mark Rivers ever made. But now he's back to make amends with Kylie and their daughter. When a health crisis draws them closer, will Mark prove he's the man his family needs...or has he lost them both for good?

A BABY IN ALASKA
Home to Hearts Bay • by Heidi McCahan

After arriving in Alaska for a wedding and business trip—with his newly orphaned baby nephew in tow—Sam Frazier knows he's in over his head. He has no choice but to accept help from feisty pilot Rylee Madden. Their arrangement is temporary, but caring for baby Silas might make their love permanent...

HER CHANCE AT FAMILY
by Angie Dicken

As the guardian of her orphaned nieces, interior designer Elisa Hartley is too busy to think about being jilted on her wedding day. *Almost.* Besides, she's already growing feelings for her new landscape architect, Sean Peters...until she discovers the secret he's been hiding.

LOOK FOR THESE AND OTHER LOVE INSPIRED BOOKS WHEREVER BOOKS ARE SOLD, INCLUDING MOST BOOKSTORES, SUPERMARKETS, DISCOUNT STORES AND DRUGSTORES.

LICNM1223

Get 3 FREE REWARDS!

We'll send you 2 FREE Books plus a FREE Mystery Gift.

FREE Value Over **$20**

Both the **Love Inspired®** and **Love Inspired® Suspense** series feature compelling novels filled with inspirational romance, faith, forgiveness and hope.

YES! Please send me 2 FREE novels from the Love Inspired or Love Inspired Suspense series and my FREE gift (gift is worth about $10 retail). After receiving them, if I don't wish to receive any more books, I can return the shipping statement marked "cancel." If I don't cancel, I will receive 6 brand-new Love Inspired Larger-Print books or Love Inspired Suspense Larger-Print books every month and be billed just $6.49 each in the U.S. or $6.74 each in Canada. That is a savings of at least 16% off the cover price. It's quite a bargain! Shipping and handling is just 50¢ per book in the U.S. and $1.25 per book in Canada.* I understand that accepting the 2 free books and gift places me under no obligation to buy anything. I can always return a shipment and cancel at any time by calling the number below. The free books and gift are mine to keep no matter what I decide.

Choose one:
- ☐ **Love Inspired Larger-Print** (122/322 BPA GRPA)
- ☐ **Love Inspired Suspense Larger-Print** (107/307 BPA GRPA)
- ☐ **Or Try Both!** (122/322 & 107/307 BPA GRRP)

Name (please print)

Address | Apt. #

City | State/Province | Zip/Postal Code

Email: Please check this box ☐ if you would like to receive newsletters and promotional emails from Harlequin Enterprises ULC and its affiliates. You can unsubscribe anytime.

Mail to the **Harlequin Reader Service:**
IN U.S.A.: P.O. Box 1341, Buffalo, NY 14240-8531
IN CANADA: P.O. Box 603, Fort Erie, Ontario L2A 5X3

Want to try 2 free books from another series? Call 1-800-873-8635 or visit www.ReaderService.com.

*Terms and prices subject to change without notice. Prices do not include sales taxes, which will be charged (if applicable) based on your state or country of residence. Canadian residents will be charged applicable taxes. Offer not valid in Quebec. This offer is limited to one order per household. Books received may not be as shown. Not valid for current subscribers to the Love Inspired or Love Inspired Suspense series. All orders subject to approval. Credit or debit balances in a customer's account(s) may be offset by any other outstanding balance owed by or to the customer. Please allow 4 to 6 weeks for delivery. Offer available while quantities last.

Your Privacy—Your information is being collected by Harlequin Enterprises ULC, operating as Harlequin Reader Service. For a complete summary of the information we collect, how we use this information and to whom it is disclosed, please visit our privacy notice located at corporate.harlequin.com/privacy-notice. From time to time we may also exchange your personal information with reputable third parties. If you wish to opt out of this sharing of your personal information, please visit readerservice.com/consumerschoice or call 1-800-873-8635. **Notice to California Residents**—Under California law, you have specific rights to control and access your data. For more information on these rights and how to exercise them, visit corporate.harlequin.com/california-privacy.

LIRLIS23